Robert Cleland

**A Rich Man's Relatives**

Robert Cleland

**A Rich Man's Relatives**

ISBN/EAN: 9783742811318

Manufactured in Europe, USA, Canada, Australia, Japa

Cover: Foto ©Andreas Hilbeck / pixelio.de

Manufactured and distributed by brebook publishing software
(www.brebook.com)

Robert Cleland

**A Rich Man's Relatives**

A

# RICH MAN'S RELATIVES.

BY

R.  CLELAND,

AUTHOR OF "INCHBRACKEN."

*IN THREE VOLUMES.*

*VOL. I.*

LONDON:

F. V. WHITE AND CO.,

31, SOUTHAMPTON STREET, STRAND, W.C.

1885.

PRINTED BY
KELLY AND CO., GATE STREET, LINCOLN'S INN FIELDS;
AND MIDDLE MILL KINGSTON-ON-THAMES.

# CONTENTS.

# A RICH MAN'S RELATIVES.

## CHAPTER I.

HOW HIS RELATIONS VEXED THE RICH MAN.

ONE evening early in July, 1858, there might have been seen through the railings of a villa in a suburban street of Montreal, if only the thick shrubbery leaves would have permitted the view, a lady—Miss Judith Herkimer, to wit —seated in a quiet corner of the verandah, and partially concealed by the clusters of a wisteria trained to the pillar against which she leaned.  Miss Judith had entered on that uninteresting middle time of life, when, though youth with its graces is undeniably of the past, the grey hairs which may perchance intrude among the brown, are not yet a crown of honour ; the bloom and the promise of life are over, but the pathetic dignity of retrospect, with its suggestions of what has or what might have been, which make age beautiful, are not yet arrived. It was the sear and dusty afternoon stage of her pilgrimage and her spinsterhood, and there was a shade of severity in her aspect, as though living had grown into something to be struggled with and endured—the season for duty to a serious mind, seeing that the time for enjoyment is manifestly gone by.

The flatness with which her hair was laid upon her temples, and then drawn back tightly without wave or pad to the apex of her head, and secured in the form of an onion, left no doubt as to the seriousness of Miss Judith's mind, while the severe ungracefulness of her dress argued an ascetic tendency of that aggressive kind which says, " Brother, I would fast, therefore you shall go without your dinner "—a person tiresome rather than bad, but with the long chin of that obstinacy which can be so provoking when the understanding and imagination are too narrow to perceive the true relation of things.

On the lawn before her stood a mulatto lad of about eighteen, dressed in the white linen suit of a house servant, and with a long apron suspended from his neck, as though he had been called from his glass-washing in the pantry.

"You say, Miss Judith," he was saying, while he pulled the apron through his fingers with a puzzled look, "dat I b'long to myself and not to de cu'nel as owns me? Den w'y dis house as you owns not b'long to me too?"

"Because property in our fellow-men is not recognized in this free country, Cato. But you cannot be expected to understand these intricate questions all at once. Patience and humility, Cato! Now for your reading. Have you got your book? Ah! yes. Here is the place. What does r a t read?"

"Cat! Miss Judy."

"Fie! Cato. *C a t* is cat. That is *rat!* Begins with an R. You see?"

"'Cep' de cat hab done gone eaten de rat. Den whaar will he be, Miss Judy? All cat after dat! I reckon."

"Cato, you are foolish! Now, attend!"

"Cato," said another voice from the back ground, "go to your pantry and assist Bridget with her tea-things," and Miss Herkimer stepped out on the verandah from a window not far off. Miss Herkimer was a good many years older than her sister, but she admitted the fact that she was elderly, and did not seem to find it interfere with her comfort. Her

1—2

hair was white, and hung in curls over her temples, and the folds of her black silk gown had a free and contented swing which refreshed the eye after the pinched exactness of Miss Judith's costume.

"Gerald and his friend have moved into the smoking-room with their cigars, and as the windows are open I was afraid your instructions might be overheard; and then, Judith, there would be a commotion which you would regret."

"We must think what is right, Susan, do it, and never mind the consequences."

"It cannot be right to interfere between our brother Gerald and his servant. If the customs in his country are different from ours, that cannot be helped. He follows his own, and while he is our guest, it is not for us to disturb."

"Think of the iniquity of slavery, Susan —that that young man should be held in bondage, in this free Canada! It seems awful. Look at him, and deny if you can that he is a man and a brother!"

"I have no objection whatever to admit his being a man and brother, but I certainly should not like to have to call him *nephew!* And that is what it may come to if you provoke Gerald. You know how violent he can be when he is roused, and if he thought we were tampering with his negro, or attempting an abolitionist scheme, he is capable even of —*adopting* him, we will call it—and leaving him his whole fortune."

" Do you think so? That would be most unprincipled conduct on his part."

" I know he is quite capable of it ; and besides, Judith, I think you are unnecessarily scrupulous about that ugly word ' slavery.' It really seems not so bad a thing after all, come to see it in action. Gerald, now, is extremely kind to the boy—spoils him, indeed, with indulgence, and makes him do very little work. How much better he is off than Stephen's foot-boy, with a pony to mind and the garden to weed when he is not splitting wood or acting butler in the house. It is Stephen's boy who is the slave, to my thinking. Again, I heard Gerald say he refused two thousand dollars for him from a barber in New Orleans. He is quite a valuable boy, and you would tempt him to leave his master !"

" Two thousand dollars for a black boy ? Why ! Stephen's white boy gets only ten dollars a month and some clothes. Does it not seem extravagant, now, to have so much money tied up in one negro ?—and sinful ?

How much good might be done with that money if the boy were realized! One like Stephen's at ten dollars a month could do his work—it seems to be only shaving his master, and after that to do what he is bid—and the rest of the money might do such very great good. Five hundred dollars might be given to African missions to enlighten his pagan fellow-countrymen, and would carry the truth to so many!—and still there would be money over to do much good."

"And how do you propose to realize a negro boy, sister, except by selling him to another slave owner? And what about the man and brother?"

"True, Susan! Quite true. I admit the force of your objection. It is another illustration of the mystery our good rector dwelt upon so touchingly last Sunday, that good and evil walk the earth hand-in-hand. A solemn thought! But in this case it really seems to me that the boy's bondage would be well compensated. He is a slave already, you must remember—has no idea what liberty means—and five hundred dollars would bring so many darkened savages within the influence of gospel light. If the poor ignorant creature knew enough to understand, I am sure he would rejoice to think that so slight a change in his own circumstances would bring so vast a benefit to his benighted brethren."

"And you'd still be fifteen hundred dollars to the good, Judith. Quite an *operation* in another man's niggers! Ha, ha! Godliness is profitable! That's sound evangelical doctrine! Ha, ha, ha!"

These words rang forth in a discordant voice from a neighbouring window, the venetians of which were now pushed open.

The ladies gasped and turned round in dismay. As they had grown earnest in their conversation their voices had been rising to the pitch at which they could not but be heard without eaves-dropping, and they had been overheard.

Within the window, which was open, stood the "Gerald" of whom they had been discoursing—a tall square-framed man, but sadly wasted and collapsed under prolonged attacks of malarial fever. He was between fifty and sixty years of age, with features which had once been stern and resolute, but now, under the stress of continued ill-health, had grown querulous and peevish in their expression. He had gone to Louisiana some thirty years before to push his fortune. From French-

speaking Lower Canada to French-understand-
ing Louisiana seemed less of an expatriation
than to English New York or California, and
such Frenchness as he was able to bring—he
was English-born after all, and only Canadian
by education—had prepossessed the Louisian-
ians in his favour. He had pushed his fortune
—married the heiress of a valuable plantation
near Natchez, where he had resided ever since
—and amassed wealth. He had lost, however,
his wife, his child, and latterly his good-health ;
and at last had been compelled to return to
his friends in the North to give his shattered
constitution a last chance to shake off the
creeping agues which were dragging him to
the grave.   He had been a year already under
his sisters' roof, greatly to his own worriment ;
for between his fever fits and the prostration
which followed them, there would intervene
hours of restless irritability, when it seemed to
him that his affairs were entangling themselves
into a knot of hopeless confusion, deprived as
they were of the master's eye which alone sees
clearly.

   "What do you think of that, major?"
Gerald continued, turning to his companion
who was gnawing the end of a very large
cigar—a tall sallow man with a much waxed
and pointed black moustache and goatee, and

an exuberant display of jewellery in his shirt front. "Who in Natchez would expect to find me summering in a nest of blazing abolitionists? Better say nothing when you get home, or I may have to settle with the vigilance committee when I go back."

"I did not expect it, colonel," said the major, pulling down his waistcoat and looking dignified. "Among fanatical Yankees I reckon on hearing the institootions of my country vilified, and so I give sech cattle a wide berth; but here, on British terri-tory, I expected some liberality. Bless my soul! trying to corrupt your servant under your very nose!"

The ladies had withdrawn in confusion under their brother's first attack, or civility to his hostesses must have kept the major silent. At the same time he felt outraged. To think that he, one of the most "high-toned" men of his neighbourhood, and with the very soundest Southern principles, should have been trapped into a den of lowlived—it was always "lowlived"—abolitionism! His friend Herkimer too, had always passed for a "high-toned gentleman" of sound principles when in Natchez, and to find him the member of such a family was inexpressibly shocking.

"Yes," said Herkimer, "it is bad—shows what fools women can be when they don't know, and swallow all the rant that gets into print. After that they think they know so much that they won't believe a word those who could tell them can say. If my boy, Cato, now, had not been an extra good nigger, these sisters of mine would have made him leave me long ago. When his mother, Amanda, died, I promised her I would always keep him about myself—and he does, I will say, understand my little ways—or I never would have ventured to bring him to Canada; but the fact is, the boy's fond of me, and won't leave me, say what they like. Still it provokes a man to see his property being tampered with. Then, too, my sister Judith feels it her dooty, she says, to speak to me about the sinfulness of having property in human beings. I ask her to prove that they *are* human, but she just rolls her eyes and looks solemn. She calls her talk ' a word in season,' but she chooses the most unseasonable times to hold forth ; generally when my chill is coming on, and the long yawn creeping up my back that we all know, when I don't feel man enough to say ' bo ' to a goose. My wig! If I could I'd say more than ' bo ' to Judith. She holds on steady till I begin to grow blue and my teeth chatter, then I pull the bell for Cato to bring more blankets, and he—good lad—always sends her away, first thing. Susan bothers too—money, generally—but I'm free to allow she has more gumption than Judith. Old maids both. That's a sort of critter we don't have down Natchez way. There they marry. Reckon you never saw any before, major? Pecoolier, ain't they?"

"The ladies are your sisters, colonel. Estimable, I doubt not; but they do not understand our Southern institootions."

"Talking of understanding, major, do you see much of my nephew, Ralph? When he went down to the plantation I gave him a letter to you, as being my nearest neighbour, and a good friend. I told him he might place implicit reliance on your opinion in any case of doubt which might arise. The overseers are men whom I could trust to make a crop if I was on the spot myself; but of course the young man had to learn, and circumstances were sure to arise in which your advice would be most val'able. Do you see him often?"

Major Considine—I omitted to mention his name earlier, and I may now add by way of making amends for the neglect, that the "*major*" was a prefix of courtesy conferred by his neighbours to describe his social status and the extent of his possessions; Herkimer's colonelcy was of the same kind, but the higher rank implied a larger holding in land and negroes—Major Considine coughed dryly, drew himself up, and looked sallower if possible than his wont, while his eyes sought the ground.

"I have seen your nephew, sir," he said, "frequently. When he came down first I invited him to come and see me, and treated him in all respects as I would any other gentleman, your friend ; but I am bound to own that lately we have not met ; " and he gave the waxed points of his moustache a further twirl with something of an aggrieved air, as if to intimate that while he had done *his* part unimpeachably, he had reason to complain of the way in which his advances had been met.

Herkimer frowned and threw away his cigar. " Fact is, major," he said, " I have a letter from Taine. Taine has been my overseer for a good many years, as you know, and I have found him a good man. He talks of leaving my employment at the end of the year, and asks me to send him a letter stating my satisfaction with him during the years he has been overseeing for me. I can well do that, but I'd hate to lose him. Good overseers are scarce. He complains that Ralph has discharged one of the assistant overseers against his wish, that he interferes with the field work, and has damaged ten of the hands to the extent of two or three hundred dollars apiece, and the crop prospect is reduced by forty or fifty bales. He says that his character for getting more bales to the hand than any other overseer in the section is at stake, and he has concluded, if I feel unable to return to the plantation, that he will leave. What do you think of it?"

"Not at all surprised, sir; Taine is not to be blamed. Mr. Ralph Herkimer came to me shortly after he had discharged that assistant you mention, to ask my advice. It seems they had met accidentally immediately after the discharge, in some saloon, and Mister Ralph Herkimer being ignorant, it appears, that in our glorious land of freedom all white men are equal, had put on some of his plantation airs. He has those plantation airs mighty strong, having, as you say yourself, knocked three or four thousand dollars off the value of your field gangs, by nothing but whipping—clear unmerciful whipping, they do say around Natchez. Waal, his tale was a good deal mixed, and I don't pretend to know the rights, but it seems the discharged overseer asked him to drink, to show he bore no spite. Mr. Ralph Herkimer refused, said something about white trash, and flung the liquor in his face. The overseer drew his pistol, and would have fired, but the folks in the bar-room interfered to protect an unarmed man, and so Mr. Ralph Herkimer rode safe home, and shortly after arriving there received a hostile message. He rode over to see me with the letter in his hand, and that is how I come to know the circumstance, colonel. And let me add, sir, that though I fear no man living, I would not have pained your feelin's by alluding to it, if you had not made it necessary yourself, by bringing up the subject. The young man showed me his letter of defiance, and I spoke to him, as an older man and a gentleman, I hope, colonel, should speak to your nephew on such an occasion. He said he was indignant at being addressed in that style by a common fellow, and that where there was no equality there could be no claim to satisfaction. I pointed out to him that under the constitootion of our State all white men are equal, and that we, the first families, were always scrupulously courteous to our poorer neighbours, that being the only way to hold the community together. We want their help often, I told him, as at election times, in case of jury trials, when their goodwill goes farther to gain a verdict than all the blathering of the lawyers ; and in case of serious trouble with the hands we can always depend on a white man, and it is well worth our while to accord him such equality as he can understand. Our first families, I told him, yield all that cheerfully, and find they can still be exclusive enough. As he had gone so far, I assured him he must fight, which after all would be a high compliment to the poor devil, and would make him—your nephew—popular with the meaner sort, which he would find profitable at an election, if by-and-by he were to naturalize and go into politics. I offered to undertake the management of the whole affair, and you are aware, colonel, I have some experience. I even showed him my French case of spring triggers, and my new patent Colt's revolvers, in case he had any preference as to arms, the choice resting with him ; and—would you believe it, sir?—but really, really I dare not call up the blush of shame on your honourable features. The—this young man—declined my offer with thanks ! He said it did not become him as a gentleman to go cut-throating with common fellows. I suggested that it was often nothing but a reverse of fortune which turned a gentleman into an assistant overseer. Then he said that bloodshed on account of a trifling misunderstanding was against his principles, when I replied that he must have mistaken Mississippi for Pennsylvania, and warned him that if he did not fight when it was put upon him, he would be insulted every time he appeared outside his own plantation. Then he asked me to use my good offices to accommodate things, but I explained to him that I could only meet the class to which his adversary belonged, either to fight them or to order them what they should do. After that Mr. Ralph Herkimer grew sulky—I thought at one time he was going to be offensive—but the pistol cases stood open on the table, and the gentleman don't like firearms I think; anyhow, he simmered down. I believe he ended by apologizing to the assistant overseer for not drinking his liquor; but I do know, I have never spoken to Mr. Ralph Herkimer since."

"I don't blame you, major," said Herkimer. "The young man is not what my father's grandson ought to be. He won't do for Mississippi, that's clear; and I ain't going to let Taine leave me on account of him. I was wise to let him go down for the first year alone, leaving his wife and child here till he knew how he liked it. He had better come home again, for *I* don't like it, whether he does or no. I had meant him to succeed me down there, major; but the man who first pays off overseers and then apologizes to them cannot do that. He is my only brother Stephen's only son. It is disappointing. My two sisters, whom you have seen, would not do for planteresses in Mississippi; but I have another sister yet—young, major, and handsome—my half-sister; just about the age of Ralph. She might be made my heiress, and if she marries as I would wish, she shall! I need not conceal the truth from myself, major. The doctors have as good as told me I shall never return to Mississippi. You have not seen her yet, Considine, this sister of mine, Mary. She is just about the age of Jeanne de Beaulieu when I married her—poor Jeanne!—not unlike her, and quite as handsome. Strange, would it not be, if Beaulieu went with an heiress again? Here comes Cato to call us into the drawing-room for tea. We'll go, Considine, if you have finished your cigar; and—who knows?—we may see Mary."

# CHAPTER II.

## STEADFAST MARY.

IT was late in November. The screen of foliage which hid the villa from the road had grown thin, changing to all gay colours, and dropping leaf by leaf. Old Gerald's health had not improved. The clear autumnal airs had failed to invigorate his fever-worn system, or brace it into vigour. They only chilled him, and forced him to keep his room.

The light was fading out of a grey and lifeless afternoon—one of those days when all things are possible, rain, frost, snow, or even a revulsion into the sunshine of a last brief remnant of St. Martin's summer, and yet nothing happens. Gerald sat by the window in his easy chair, wrapped in a thick dressing-gown and buried under many rugs. His letters lay at his elbow unread, and the *New Orleans Picayune* was on his lap, but he was too listless to look into its contents. His eyes were turned towards the road, and he watched with as much impatience as his torpid faculties were capable of feeling.

"There she is at last!" he muttered after a while. "Glad! She is all the company I have now, or can expect while I am kept indoors. Susan and Judith don't count in that way, even if they tried to be agreeable, which they don't. The one is for ever bothering about my negroes and my soul, the other about my money. What have I done that they should imagine they may puzzle their foolish heads over me and my affairs, or wag their cackling tongues. I am sick, and want nursing, so they take me for a child? Think of me, who consult no one, being advised by *them!* But never mind, here is little Mary. She is always good company, and she never bothers."

"But who is the fellow walking with her? Big and strapping. Fair hair, whiskers and moustache—not bad to look at, but seems most unnecessarily eager in his attentions. Wonder who he is. Carrying her music? Very proper; but he need not linger so long before letting go her hand. Mary shouldn't let him—looks particular—the major would not like that."

Presently Mary entered the room. She was flushed, or perhaps the air had heightened her complexion and brightened her eyes, which shone like stars; and there were smiles lingering about her lips, in wait, as it were, to break forth again on the first pretext.

"Your walk has done you good," said Gerald. "Where have you been? I have been wearying for you to come home; but now one sees you, it is impossible to grudge your short constitutional, you are so brightened up by it. I wish Considine was here to see you."

"I have been at choir-practising. I promised to take the solo in Sunday's anthem, and have been trying it over. The booming of the organ through the empty church rouses one, I think. I generally feel brighter after it, and that may account for my looking so cheerful as you say."

"And who is the gentleman who carried home your music?"

"That is Mr. Selby, our organist. A splendid player. If you had not been such an invalid, you would have known both his playing and himself ere now."

"It would seem that you know him very well; and to see you walking together one would have said that he knows you very well too. You appear quite intimate, and yet I have never seen him here."

" No. Susan will not let him be invited to the house. She says his is not a recognized profession. As if a successful musician were not better than a bungling doctor or notary! It has something to do with the *line* which she says must be drawn—between wholesale and retail, for instance—if Montreal is to have a Society. A ridiculous line, it seems to me, which excludes many wealthy and accomplished people as traders, while it lets in poor Stephen and his wife, with her superfluous h's, because his little business in needles and pins is wholesale, seeing that he never sells less than a thousand at a time."

" Mrs. Stephen is my sister-in-law, and may do with her h's what she pleases. It is not her fault if she was born in the British metropolis, and if Stephen is not in opulent circumstances, it is just because it has so happened. I have known many high-toned families who were but in a small way *pecooniarily* speaking. I am surprised to hear you run Stephen and his family down, though I confess I have been disappointed myself in his son Ralph."

" I don't run them down; but why should they be so particular about others? It was Mrs. Stephen who said to Susan that an organist wasn't ' genteel,'—Mrs. Stephen, who doesn't know one tune from another—and so Mr. Selby has never been asked to the house. And then Judith chimed in with her ' higher grounds.' She says that good music is a snare and device of the High Church party, and that you got on very well without it long ago in the old church at Stoke-upon-Severn. A funny church it must have been."

" So it was, and I reckon you would not have liked it. The village joiner and the bellows mender played the clarionet and the bassoon in a little loft over the squire's pew, while the blacksmith's daughter sang the hymns, and the schoolmaster as clerk said the responses out loud before the people. But the world has changed since then. Yes ! I daresay an organist might do as well to invite as anybody else. But what does it matter? What do you want with an organist? You have no organ."

" I like to be able to invite my friends just as other people do. If you knew him, Gerald, you would like him."

" I dare say. There are many people one would like if one knew them. Yet if one does not, it seems of little consequence, there are so many others. If you lived in Natchez, now, you would not see much of your Canadian friends. You would make friends down there, and very high-toned and elegant you would find them."

"Natchez, Gerald? What should I be doing there?"

"Doing? Living, of course; surrounded by every elegance that money and the best society can secure. If I live and get well, it is my intention to carry you back with me, and make you mistress of the Beaulieu estate— de Bully they call it for short. In case I do not, and I can see the doctor has not much hope of my recovery, I have willed the place and all my property to you. Don't stare, Mary. It is so. I feel it a duty to provide a good mistress for those helpless creatures who are dependent on me, and you, I am satisfied, will be that. I have tried Ralph, as you know, and have found him unfit to take my place. You are the only other member of the family who could go there. You will marry, and the plantation will prosper. Treat the poor creatures kindly, Mary. But I know you will, and Considine is an excellent manager. His place adjoins ours. You will have the finest estate for miles on that part of the river."

"Oh! This seems very strange to me."

"You will get used to it in time. But to tell you the truth, I did not think the idea would be altogether new to you. I did not think Considine would have been so backward. He must be hard hit to be so diffident of his success in taking a girl's fancy. Has he said nothing to you?"

"It would have been strange in Major Considine to have divulged your testamentary intentions. You surely do not think he would speculate to me about your chances of recovery, or what you would do with your property. I should have stopped him at once if he had mooted the subject, you may be sure."

"I did not suppose that he had divulged my intentions, but I think it is about time that he had declared his own. After visiting here so constantly all through the summer, and keeping you singing by the hour to him downstairs in the drawing-room, he has surely made himself understood. Still, I wonder he has not spoken. Not that I have a right to complain, he has declared himself plainly enough to *me*, or you may be sure I would have put a stop to his visits long ago. Still I wonder at his backwardness. Where are you running to, Mary? Has he said nothing?"

"I want to take off my things," said Mary, her face aflame with blushes.

"Tell me before you go. What has he said? Tell me! There is his ring at the front door. I must speak to him."

"I don't know. But better say nothing," cried Mary in evident confusion, escaping from the room.

Gerald would have recalled her, but the major's heavy step was already audible on the stairs. He could only throw |himself back in his chair with an impatient snort.

"Colonel!" said Considine, entering, "I come to make you my *adieux*"— 'adoos' is how he pronounced it, the Major was certainly not French. "What orders for Taine at the plantation? Any commands for any one down there? I shall be pleased to be your messenger. I see by the Memphis paper there was a slight touch of frost the other night, so the sickly season is over, and I can safely go home to look after my affairs. They want looking into, I reckon, after five months' absence. I have to thank you for the very pleasant summer I have put in here."

"Do you mean it, major? Going right off? I have reckoned on your being here till the New Year."

"The call to go home has come sudden, colonel, but I reckon I had best obey it."

"And what about our plan to join the plantations?"

"I'm agreeable, colonel—anxious I should say; but if the lady ain't, what can I do?"

"You don't know, major, till you try.    I reckon a sister of mine ain't just like a ripe persimmon, to drop in a man's mouth before he shakes the tree."

"Shakes the tree, colonel?    There ain't no man ever shook the tree harder than I did. I shook in both my shoes for a mortal hour before I could steady my voice—that shook too—enough to say what I wanted.    All the time I was trying, the lady was diverting herself with her singing.    French songs, and I-talian songs, full of all kind of rare fandangoes, like a mocking bird in a cherry tree. I couldn't get a word in endways for ever so long, and when I did, at last, she just stopped and looked at me out of her eyes.    And when I got through, she said 'Oh! Mr. Considine, it's all a mistake.    You have misunderstood, and I don't understand.    I am quite sure I cannot say what you desire, so we will suppose that you have not asked me to, and that nothing has been said at all, and we will agree never to recur to the subject.' And then she asked me if I did not think the last movement in the song she had been singing very effective, and the bravura passage at the end powerfully written.    By-and-by I got away.    You may suppose she did not play a great deal more music, and that I had got about enough for that time. I ain't a widower, colonel, as you know; I never was refused before, and I never backed out of an engagement, so you may say that I have no experience in these matters; but it appears to me that the young lady knows her own mind, and there is no use in my speaking to her again."

"But she didn't know about the joining our plantations then. I had only just done explaining that to her when you came in, and she ran out, which shows that she ain't indifferent to the idea, as who in their senses could be? The two will make a mighty pretty property, and you and Mary will look well at the head of it, and raise a fine family to come after you. She did not know she was heir to my property when she took you down that time. Ha, ha, major! It makes me laugh to think of it. You that so long have been boss of the range, and had only to beckon to fetch any gal in all the country— you to come all the way to Canada to be took down by a gal that didn't know she had a dollar to her name!"

"Sir, the subject of your jests is not a pleasant one. Let us pass on."

"I ask your pardon, major. No offence was intended; but if you will speak to Mary now,

I am willing to bet any money her answer will be different. A man of experience should not mind every word a young woman says, when it is about marrying. It is the one time in life she is let have her head, and we must not blame her for taking it, just at first. Trust me, she has thought better of it already. Try again."

"It would be useless, colonel."

"Don't give in, sir! If the gal and the plantation are to your liking, that is."

"I think a mighty deal of the lady, sir; and would be fain to repeat my offer, even if she were as much without fortune as she believed herself to be last night; but I do not see my way to doing so after what has passed between us, the more so that now my fortune —a mighty neat one though it be—will count for less than before, seeing she knows now how well you have provided for her."

"I believe that will influence her the other way. However, it is reasonable you should want to halt and take breath before returning to the attack. This is a disappointment to me, but I won't cry beat yet, if you are still minded to persevere. Let me speak to her, and I will write to you. Now the ice has been broken between you, you will be able to take up the subject by letter."

Considine shortly took his leave, and Gerald awaited the return of Mary, who did not appear till Cato had been sent to hammer on her chamber door and request her presence.

"Is this true," said Gerald, when she at length entered the room, "which I hear of you? Have you really gone and said 'No' to Considine's proposal? Do you know that he owns a hundred and fifty head of the likeliest niggers in all the Mississippi Valley, besides land and sundries?—nigh on two hundred thousand dollars, and no debts. What do you expect to be able to catch if Considine ain't good enough for you?"

"I didn't say he was not good enough. He deserves a better wife than I could make him, and I believe he will have no difficulty in finding her."

"But it is in you he thinks he has found her, Mary! Don't be foolish, you are not likely ever to get a better offer, or another half as good. The man is steady and well off, a kind man and a perfect gentleman. What more would you have?"

"I do not want more, Gerald! But then I do not want—him."

"What is your objection to him? Is it his appearance, or his temper, or what? Is he not passably well-looking?"

"I would almost call him handsome."

"Does he not succeed in making himself sufficiently agreeable to you? I can assure you, at any rate, that you have succeeded in being agreeable to him. He says he would be fain to get you if you had not a cent to your name. Can a man say more than that?"

"I do not know that he can."

"Then what is your fault to him?"

"I find no fault with him. On the contrary——"

"Then why won't you marry him?"

"Because I could not like him in that way."

"What can a girl like you know about the marrying way?"

"I know that I could not marry Mr. Considine."

"Why? Is there some one else?"

Mary's face flushed hotly and her eyes fell.

"Ha! Have I caught you? You are engaged already? Why did you never tell? Surely you might have trusted your big brother. You never saw me till the other day, it is true, but we have been fast friends for twelve months now, have we not, Mary? Why did you never tell me?" And he drew her towards him as he spoke, and kissed her on the forehead. "Think I feel no interest in my future heir?"

"Because, Gerald, you do not know him. How could I tell you?"

"Tell me now, then, dear. Who is he?"

"You must find out," she answered with a watery smile and changing colour. "Girls are not expected to say such things, because they cannot."

"You say I do not know him? Have I seen him?"

"Yes."

"Do I know him by sight? Or have I seen him recently?"

"Yes, very recently indeed—as recently as could be."

"What? Then—you do not say? But it cannot be, Mary?"

There was a self-convicted look in Mary's face which pleaded guilty to the unspoken indictment.

"Do you really mean—but no, you cannot mean your friend the organist?"

Mary bowed her head in silence and looked expectantly in her brother's face, till his rising colour and the gathering frown left no doubt as to his reception of her tidings; then she removed her eyes with a heavy sigh and let them fall on the carpet.

" You cannot mean it, Mary? You!—my father's daughter!—my sister!—to engage yourself to marry a kind of fiddler!"

" He is *not* a fiddler, in your sense, Gerald, although he can play the violin, and indeed most other instruments. He is a cultured person, and has his university degree— Bachelor of Music—while few of those who try to look down on him have had the chance even to get plucked for one, having never gone to college at all."

" He plays tunes at any rate in a church loft on Sundays for a living. Is that a fit occupation for the man who would marry my sister?"

" Remember the great composers, Gerald. More than one of them was a chapelmaster, which is just an organist."

" The great fiddlesticks! If you had seen them in their lifetime in their frowzy little German houses and dirty linen, with their wives cooking their dinner, such as it was, for there was little enough at times to put in the pot, you would think less of their greatness. What good is the greatness which is not found out till after you are dead? A great fortune! That is the only greatness a sensible woman will marry to."

" Shame, Gerald! You do not mean what

you say. You have been married yourself, and I know you loved and honoured your wife. Do you mean now to say that your wife was a fool because she married you when you were not rich? Or is it that she was mercenary and married you for your money?"

"Tush! Mary. You never saw poor Jeanne, so you cannot speak about her. The beautiful darling!" Gerald's voice grew husky here, and there was some coughing before he could resume.

"No! She was not mercenary, and she was not a fool. She married me when I was a poor man because we loved one another, and she did not think about money. But if she had, it was not an unwise thing, as it turned out, which she did in marrying me, for I managed her property successfully, and more than doubled its value."

"Then why will you doubt that another woman—and she your own sister—may love as well, or that the man she intrusts her future to, may be as well able as you were to take care of it? Mr. Selby has a great many pupils, and can very well maintain a wife."

"A wife, I dare say, but not my sister. It is true my property which I intend you to have is far more than Jeanne had when she married me ; but I was able to take care of her and of what she had, and the property throve in my hands. An organist is different. What could such as he do with a gang of unruly niggers? It needs a clear business head and a strong arm to make plantation property pay."

"He does not aspire to your property, Gerald. He does not know of it, and with his feelings I am not sure that he would consent to become a slave-owner."

"Not consent, eh? Never fear. His consent will not be asked, for mine shall never be given to his owning my negroes. Slave-owning forsooth! No. Let him manage his chest of whistles. I have no right and no wish to dictate to you, though I would dearly like to see you marry Considine ; but at least I can make sure, and I will, that your insidious organgrinder shall never benefit a cent by my money, I promise you that, and I shall alter my will accordingly."

# CHAPTER III.

## LITTLE ARCADIA.

FOUR years later, and summer once more. Again it is in a suburban garden, not a very extensive one, but nicely kept; inclosed by tall trees and dense shrubbery on every side, and disclosing nothing of what may stand beyond, but here and there the corner of a chimney intruding its morsel of red amongst the sunny green of the tree-tops ,and the golden cross on the neighbouring steeple soaring over all, and shining down its benediction on the peace below.

The grass is as short, soft, and green as constant mowing and sprinkling and warmth can make it. The flower-beds are masses of brilliant colour, and in the centre stands the house, a tin-roofed wooden cottage painted in the whitest white, relieved by vividly green venetians; a broad verandah round the whole, windows descending to the floor, and above, small casements peering out through the shin-

ing tin, each with its venetian thrown open to
admit the breeze which comes up at the de-
cline of day. The effect is cool, and home-
like, notwithstanding the keenness of the
colours, and quite other than that of the raw-
toned packing-boxes in which so many an
American is condemned to pass the night, and
from which he is in so great a hurry to escape
in the morning. It may be merely a pecu-
liarity in the pitch of a French Canadian roof,
or it may be some spiritual association which
lingers about the work of these first settlers
and oldest inhabitants; but there is a personality, permanence, and history about the newest
and frailest of their structures which is want-
ing in the buildings of their English speaking
neighbours, even when they give permanence
to vulgar commonplace by embodying it in
brick or stone.

The pillars of the verandah are garlanded
with roses—pink, crimson, white, and creamy
yellow—blooming profusely, but, to judge from
the ruin of shed petals scattered on the ground,
soon to cease. Already, however, clematis—
white, purple, blue—has begun to appear and
will be ready to catch up the song of the roses,
though in a minor key, so soon as their colour
harmonies shall fade out. Butterflies are flut-
tering in the scented air, and a humming bird

flits here and there where the flowers are thickest.

In a garden seat is Mary—no longer Herkimer, but Selby, now—and at her feet is a child, something more than a year old, who rolls and kicks upon the grass, crowing and babbling the while in a language which only mothers understand. Mary looks no older than she did in her brother's sick-room; fresher, perhaps, and fuller of harmonious life, as well may happen where the desires were reasonable and are all fulfilled. She is mistress of her own life, and of his in whom she trusts, as well as of that other at her feet, in whom his and hers are united and bloom anew; and as for the life, she would not wish it to be other than it is, even if it were in her power to change it. She is at work upon some small matter of muslin and lace which busies her fingers, while it leaves her thoughts free to wander; and their wanderings are among pleasant places, to judge by her smile and the big full breath of utter content.

The winter which was coming on when we saw Gerald last proved more than his enfeebled system could bear up against; he died before it was out; and Mary, feeling that her duty at home was accomplished, and seeing no good reason to sacrifice herself to the family prejudices, took her fate in her own hands and married the man of her choice.

"And it has all turned out so beautifully," she was saying to herself with a well-pleased sigh, when the click of the gate latch roused her from her reverie. It was Selby with his roll of music. She rose to meet him, and they made the round of their domain together, observing what new buds had opened since yesterday, and telling each other the events of the day.

"I heard a man down town say that your nephew Ralph is succeeding most wonderfully since he dropped the law and turned broker."

"I am glad of that, George. Poor Ralph! It was hard upon him the way Gerald seemed to take him up at first—sending him down to live upon the property at Natchez, and letting him expect to inherit it—and then to recall him and drop him so suddenly. He refused to see him even, when he came home. Judith says it was Colonel Considine set him against Ralph, to make him leave everything to me. But I do not think that. I always found Colonel Considine 'very much of a gentleman,' to use his own expression—a little high-backed and tiresome, no doubt, but incapable of a shabbiness like that.

What good would it have done him my getting everything, considering how little we saw or cared for each other?"

"Speak for yourself, Mary. I am not so sure that Considine's interest in you was slight. From little things you have said I suspect—Nay, never blush for that, dearest, though the crimson is infinitely becoming —Having gained the prize I am not churl enough to resent another's having wished for it. Indeed, knowing as I do now how much he has missed, I could feel sorry for him, and I cannot but respect his good taste. I really could not believe that he attempted to undermine Ralph in his uncle's favour ; a thing, by-the-way, which Ralph, according to those who know him best, is well able to do for himself; he has so many crooked little ways, and is proud of them, and careless about concealment, because I suppose it does not strike him that they can shock people, or are at all out of the way—obtuseness of moral perception, I fancy, it might be called."

"And yet, George, he was the only one of the family who did not oppose our marriage, and who has not given me up utterly, ever since. Surely that shows a good heart. I, at least, shall always think kindly of Ralph for that, if for nothing else."

"My good innocent darling! Do you not see that that manœuvre alone, if there were nothing else, would stamp the man as selfish and a schemer? Remember the terms of your brother's will. He names you as his heiress, but he provides against contingencies which he fears may arise. He does not leave the property to you, but to Jordan the notary, and Considine, as trustees. In case you married Considine the trust was at an end, and everything passed to you at once. If you did not, all was to be sold and the money invested in Canada bank-stock and other securities which he named. You were to have the interest while you remained single or married with the approval of Mr. Jordan, in accordance with written instructions left in his hands. If you married contrary to these instructions, however, you were to receive nothing. The interest and dividends were to be re-invested as they fell due, and at the end of twenty years from your brother's death the whole is to be divided among your children, share and share alike; and in case you have none it is to go to Ralph's boy. Everything is tied up with only an annuity of a thousand dollars each to his three sisters and his brother. Now! Do you recognize the true inwardness of Ralph's amiability? "

" And pray, sir " cried Mary, drawing back with eyes wide open, " How come you to know all this? I would have bitten my tongue out sooner than tell you. It seems so ungenerous in Gerald to have treated you so."

"It shows the generosity of Gerald's sister, and that is all I care for. But often, I will own it, my conscience has reproached me with depriving you of your splendid inheritance; only, we are so happy here; and if love can make up for money—if my love——"

" Hush, George! I have all I want—more, I think sometimes, than should fall to one woman's share—and I wonder if it can last. But who told you about the will?"

" Who but your sister Judith! "

" She? I did not think you knew her; and she spoke so unkindly when I proposed to bring and introduce you. You surprise me."

" Ah! Miss Judy is a woman of surprises —a woman of energy who does not stick at trifles; and she is a diplomatist. She would not let you introduce me, that would have been yielding you a point; but she could find

me out for herself when she wished to spea
to me. That was on what she consider
business, and did not oblige her to know m
next time we met. It would have forced *m*
to know *her* afterwards, if she had wished it .
but that is nothing. Where would be the gai
in being a lady, if rules worked both ways
Miss Judy found me out, and requested a few
minutes' private conversation in the most
gracious way possible. She apologized pro
fusely for the intrusion, with quite a pretty
warming of the complexion and an engaging
little twitter behind her glove tips. Ass
that I was, I grew red like a lobster all over
my face, and my heart thumped against my
ribs like a smithy hammer. I imagined your
family were relenting towards me—that piety
and true principle had overcome in the
second Miss Herkimer her disapproval of our
attachment, and that she had come to tell me
so. I could have knelt down and kissed her
hand, so overcome was I with grateful joy.
It was well I did not. The group would have
been too ridiculous. Miss Judy appealed to
my feelings as a gentleman and a man of
honour ' not to ruin the prospects of her
sweet young sister ; ' that was her phrase, and
she rendered it in a fine adagio manner,
accompanied by a tremolo of her crumpled

pocket-handkerchief, which did her artistic instinct the greatest credit, and really made the little petition seem both reasonable and affecting. Judy would have succeeded on the stage, Mary, I do believe, if they had put her in training early."

"George, you are profane. It sounds ribald to speak of serious people in that way."

"Judy and the playhouse, eh? It *is* a little incongruous, I admit; but which has most right to resent the juxtaposition we need not stop to inquire. Miss Judith told me you had come into a large fortune, and your family were anxious about your matrimonial prospects, so many swells were your friends, and you were so highly connected. There was at least one general officer and a captain of dragoons, besides many more; but whether they wanted to marry you, or were only your grandfather's cousins, I did not quite catch. You see my feelings were a little tumultuous, like those of the man stepping on board a steamboat to meet his sweetheart, when he misses the plank and drops into the water. I had a feeling of cold bath all over, and was cross, I dare say; at least I did not respond to Miss Judy's condescensions as she had expected. At once she changed her tone, drawing herself up and looking

severely superior. It was scarcely con-
ceivable, she told me with dignified coldness,
that I could seriously have expected anything
more than a little notoriety would result
from my appearing in public conversing with
her sister, but if I cherished any delusion on
the subject, it was for my good that she
should speak plainly, and as a Christian she
saw it her duty to do so. It was out of the
question, she told me, that you should marry
a man in my position, and one who was not
a gentleman. This to me, whose gentlemanly
feelings she had just been appealing to! It
sent the blood tingling down to my finger-
tips, and revived me after the *douche* of what
she had been saying before. I told her these
were matters I declined to discuss with a
lady whom I had not the honour of being
acquainted with, and that while I enjoyed
the privilege of your friendship, none but
yourself should dictate to me the terms.
Then she pulled out a paper which she said
was a copy of your brother Gerald's will, and
another, the private instructions he had left
with Jordan. She insisted on reading them
both to me, word by word, and was especially
emphatic in her rendering of the instructions
in which I am mentioned by name as a person
you were not to marry."

"I know, George; and I think it was cruel in Gerald to make such a stipulation. However, it does not matter. I did not want the money, and you do not grudge to earn money for us both; and what do we want which we have not got?"

"True, my darling; and after all, your dividends which fell due before you disobeyed your kinsman's commands by marrying me have bought us this cosey little home, so you did not come to me a penniless bride after all. Talking of these things, by-the-way, reminds me—Did you observe Considine's name in the war news this morning? He is a general now. Why, Mary, you might have been one of their great ladies down there, if you had chosen!"

"But I did not choose; and I question if a general's lady down there has much to congratulate herself on. Grant is in Memphis, I see, and steadily working southwards. The negroes on the plantations are in a ferment, and Mrs. Dunwiddie, the refugee who is staying with Mrs. Brown, and called here to-day, says the boxes of silver spoons and candlesticks the Yankee officers are sending home to their friends by express are more than the Express Company's car will carry, and they talk of requisitioning a gunboat to carry their loot

North to Cincinnati. I should not have liked to ride with my plate and valuables in an ambulance in the rear of even a husband's column. But is it not fortunate that Gerald's property was realized, and the money received safely in Canada before these troubles began? You and I may not be the richer for it, but think of Edith, the little elf; what a sum it will be when she is old enough to receive it!"

"Over a million of dollars. Far too much for a girl to have. Let us hope she may have brothers and sisters to share it with. But where, at the same time, have you left this great heiress? I have not had a chance yet to give her a kiss."

"I called Lisette to come for her when you came in. Ah! There she is, among the raspberry bushes—ruining her white frock with berry juice, I'll be bound, for it is Cato who is carrying her. See how she clutches his curly wool while he picks fruit for her. Her tugging must be quite sore, but he seems positively to enjoy it, he is so fond of her."

"And well he may. Have you forgot Judith's and Ralph's attempt to ' *realize* ' him when his master died?—to huddle him over to Buffalo and sell him into slavery again. Miss Judith thought she could do so much good with the money, and Ralph encouraged

:, and undertook to arrange the transaction
the American side, when he would quietly
.e pocketed the money, I make no doubt.
ou had not interfered and explained things
the poor boy he certainly would have
en into their trap, and been disposed of for
h down. He is the only decent nigger I
r saw, and the only one who could have
·n so imposed on. Oh, yes! He would do
ything for you or the child."

· Dinner will be on the table almost at
e, George. Come in and get ready."

· Ah, yes! Dinner and something cool,
.r the long broiling day. By-and-by, when
: candles are lit, and the moths and beetles
ne droning in from the darkness to singe
ir wings in the flame, we will have music
l a little singing. Some of those dear old
gs by the masters we used to revel in long
). Haydn and the rest. Such as 'Gra-a-
ful partner.'"

· Quite so, your highness. That I may
e to respond 'Spouse adorèd,' my most
reign lord and master! Ha, ha, ha!
at it is to be a lord of creation! Mean-
le, there is the bell. Hurry to your
m."

# CHAPTER IV.

## " OUFF."

THE hour which saw Mary Selby thus lapping herself in her simple joys, was the same which witnessed the brewing of the storm destined to wreck and scatter them. A premonition must have been upon her spirits—that impalpable tremor and exhilaration preceding a catastrophe which whets the perceptions to intenser enjoyment before the destroying assault, like advancing fire which illumines, expands, and glorifies ere it leaps on its prey and turns it into smoke and ashes. It is certain at least that her spirits overstepped the limit of their tranquil wont. She turned over the piles of music with her husband in search of something to sing, but the measured graces of the older works were all too serious for her mood.

"Your masters are prosy, George," she cried; " I could not settle down to sing them

to-night. Let us have that new duet from
the "Grand Duchesse."

"From Bach to Offenbach," he answered.
"What a leap! You really are exuberant
to-night. What next?"

Five or six miles away, on the lake-like
broadening of the river which stretches upward from Lachine, a canoe was drifting
under the lee of the wooded islands, and in
it sat Ralph Herkimer. Remaining in town
through the summer to watch the fluctuations
of the gold-room—it was during the American war—he betook himself each afternoon
to Lachine, to exchange the dust of streets
for the breezy coolness of the water. He
had been fishing, and Paul, an Indian from
the Indian village of Caughnawaga near by,
managed the canoe. His fishing had not
prospered. It seemed indifferent to him,
indeed, whether he got "bites" or not, but
still from time to time he made a cast of the
line, with his eyes brooding on the water
where the slackened current drifted lazily
by, with its rhythmic ripples flickering in
the reddening light. The sun went down
behind heavy banks of cloud, and the grey
twilight stole silently up with that listening
stillness which makes audible the murmur

of the stream, a sound unnoticed in the garish hurry of noon when the world is vocal with a hundred noises, but heard at eve when other things with life have sunk to sleep.

The canoe hung idly among the gathering shadows of the shore where the waters were black and oily in the shelter of the wooded islands; but Ralph took no heed of the twilight closing in. The coolness, the drowsy movement, and the murmur soothed him, and his thoughts flowed freely in their wonted channels. They were like the streams we read of which run over golden sands, for they were all about money, shares, stocks, margins, shorts, longs, bulling and bearing the market, with sunny visions of a hundred per cent. glittering remotely, like islands of the blest, and with banks of contingency drifting in between. Then his memory wandered to the fortune he had missed, and which should surely have been left to him, his father's only son, and the only male shoot of the family tree. To think of so much money being deliberately left past him! — tied up for twenty years to wait for heirs unborn at the time of Gerald's death. He snorted and moved restlessly in his seat as he thought of it, till the jerking of his limbs disturbed the unstable equilibrium of the canoe, and he only composed and controlled himself in time to avoid a ducking from the rolling over of the lightly-poised craft. Paul raised his hand and caught the water with his paddle at the same instant, relapsing into his impassive wont so soon as the accident was averted.

"Too bad!" muttered Ralph, when the disturbance of his nerves had subsided, and his thoughts fell back into their channel. "If the old man would none of me personally, there was my boy, and he bears his name and is a Herkimer—nearer to him, surely, than the music master's brat; and she a girl, too, as it turns out!" Then his thoughts grew deep again—sank into silence, as the rivers in a limestone country disappear into the ground, and thread mysterious miles through caves of night and blackness.

He whipped the waters with his line, letting it drift anon and forgetting to draw it in even when an infatuated bass caught hold and jerked and struggled till he got away again, and even the apathetic Paul looked up surprised; but then, the ways of the pale faces are not as those of the red man, so he merely grunted, and became quiescent again as before.

4—2

"Too bad!" Ralph muttered again. "Only a life between my boy and a million!—it will be nearer three millions by the end of the twenty years—just one life between my Gerald and all that; and what a life! Only a year old—incapable of knowing anything about it, or taking any satisfaction out of it. A girl, too, at that. Child of an organ-grinder. Nobody worth knowing will ever care to know her. Of what use can a million of dollars be to such as she?" Here with a groan and a snort the black waters of unwholesome thought sunk down again out of sight, and out of ken of the thinker, if that were possible, for—under the devil's guidance shall we call it?—one will sometimes avert the eyes from the working and festering of his own soul with a sense of conventional shame (hypocrisy is like the polar frosts which strike a yard or two down into the ground), and still with the back turned as it were to the evil thought, as a man must continue to do within himself if he would retain his own good opinion, there will be a furtive peering glance cast down and backward into the deeper depths, awaiting till some deeper down conscience is overcome, which is not the admitted self at all, yet the vanquishment of which will be so

good an excuse for dropping the moral
barriers in the upper stratum of admitted
consciousness. To that wave of unstem-
mable temptation, a cyclone as it were to
which nature in her strength succumbs,
and the best of men may yield, lifting their
heads again after it, like palm trees when
the tempest has passed over, and saying,
"A storm; a convulsion beyond human
might to withstand; for yielding to that,
who can be blamed? Let us spread our
draggled plumage wide to dry. The gale
is over, and we shall soon be as honorable
as before."

Not that Ralph could be called a hypo-
crite in the vulgar sense. For why? He
troubled himself little about morals of any
kind, that not being, as he said, his particular "fad." But there is a righteous-
ness which is not ecclesiastical. There are
decencies of life for us all, and a standard of
right and wrong, which it is *base* to contra-
vene even when we put on speculative
airs and question the Church's teachings.
Right is always right, and wrong wrong,
decency decent, and baseness contemptible,
even if there were no God in heaven,
and no account to render at the last day;
and there are thoughts which a man must

turn his back on when they pass through his mind, if he would continue to enjoy his own respect.

There is a way of seeing sidewise, however, when the eyes are averted—a policy of reconciliation between doing and eschewing, when deeds at once vile and profitable are under consideration—and I fear me much this luckless Ralph Herkimer had found out the trick of it.

His thoughts, at all events, sank down deep into those sunless channels where even he himself declined wittingly to follow them though keeping watch. He whipped the water more briskly than before, and stared intently at the end of his line; but somehow he did not lose the thread of his reflections; he kept on thinking all the time and even with more and more intentness, though still he made pretence to himself of ignoring the whole of the deep-down discussion—till it was finished, that is—then he succumbed, as who may not, under sufficient temptation? It is a question of price or number. Ralph yielded before the flashing glory of *millions of dollars!* So Danæ may have stretched her arms, erewhile so chaste and cold, to welcome Jove when drest in that disguise he sought the mer-

cenary maid. Was not gold divine? And
has it not continued ever since to be the
same? Even Miss Judy can appraise to a
cent the good to be achieved with part in
saving souls, and still leave unexpressed the
balance—the pride and finery which what re-
mains will bring the priests and priestesses of
Goody.

Millions of dollars! That was the burden
and refrain which repeated itself over and
over in Ralph's mind; and it ought by
right to be his. Was not he grandson of the
father of this childless Gerald who had made
the money? The only grandson too, and the
only person through whom future generations
of Herkimers could connect themselves with
this fortune? And Gerald to pass him over!
Gerald who talked so much about Shropshire,
and all the rest of it, things of which he
(Ralph) knew nothing—old Uncle Gerald
who would not hear, even, of Aunt Mary's
marrying a music master. That the old
man's money should be tied up for twenty
years and then handed over to this very music
master's brats. Gerald could not have meant
it; notwithstanding the little unpleasantness
which occurred when he (Ralph) returned from
Natchez, and Gerald refused to admit him to
his presence. The bequest must have been

merely a threat which the imprudent old man
had supposed so terrible that nobody would
brave it.  If he could have dreamed that Mary
would defy him, and marry all the same, he
would have made a different disposition of his
property altogether.    What he meant was to
go on governing his relations after death as
he had ruled them while in life.

There seemed at the moment a pathos
to this hard and worldly-minded Ralph,
swinging and oscillating silently in the
fading light, with air and tinted greyness
all around, and only the heaving, quivering
reflections upon which he swung beneath ;
there seemed a pathos in it, and he felt a
sympathy with the vanished and disappointed maker of the fortune, or rather with
the straying misdirected wealth.  If he had
lived, how different all would have been ; and
Ralph looked out into the empty evening air,
feeling as if he might catch some shadowy
glimpse of a disembodied presence, which
would look on him friendly-wise, and which he
would have greeted—oh, so reverently !—the
revisiting shadow of a millionaire, come back
regretfully to make amends to an illused
relative whom the glamour of life and the flesh
had led him to misjudge.  Ralph felt he could
meet his uncle in a fitting spirit, friendly, for-

giving, and open to any suggestions the other
state might have enlightened him to make; for
was he not doing his best to remedy the un-
fortunate and injudicious dispositions of the
will? Had he not already taken the best
advice in the province to remedy them, and
been told that the will was good, sure, fast, and
without flaw—that it would stand, and there
was no remedy?

He peered far off into the shadows, and
around on either hand. There was nothing
but a gradual failing in the light—neither sound
nor vision—only, over against him, let the
canoe turn as it might, there sat the Indian
Paul, an image brown and still, with dull,
quiescent eyes, gazing into nowhere, ready at
a moment to flash into fire and life, but absent
until wanted; plainer than the unseen vision
in his thoughts, yet less to be understood—a
mute and dusky image of the unknowable.
The dark unwinking eyes gleamed with no
thought or intelligence; they looked out
seemingly beyond, and burned, or rather
smouldered, like coals abstracted from the
nether fire, awaiting the gust of passion
to rouse the slumbering blaze. Black like
the mirrors used by necromancers, they
showed back, when he looked in them,
his own soul stripped of conventional trap-

pings, looking out of them into himself, and
seeming to have gathered active evil in their
dusky depths—a wish to guide the dubious
hand of Fate which deals the cards promiscu-
ously as though her eyes were bandaged, and
influence the falling of the aces and kings,
just one place now and then to the right or
left.   We would all like to do that, if we could
—just a little—and bring out more clearly as
we think, the poetical justice of Time ; but it
comes right in the end, of itself, without our
help, and "if it tarry," as the Prophet says,
" wait for it ; " it is for the best.

Ralph is impatient, however ; and it is not,
besides, poetic justice that he is thinking of.
Nothing so abstract.   It is money, good and
lawful coin of the realm, and it is himself and
his children, he thinks, who should have it.
Gerald, too, he takes it, having attained to
that clearer insight which is gained beyond
the grave, must wish it likewise, and if the inheritance under that most pernicious will can
be turned aside, he feels that he will be fulfilling
the present and maturer wishes of the testator.
The law may say otherwise ; but what of the
law ?   There is a higher law !   We have all
heard of it, though generally, let us hope,
when the issue was unconnected with the pos-
session of dollars.   Gerald must have heard of

the higher law. Here was a case involving
money, and when one comes to money what
is more sacred? The forger "gets twenty
years" for his crime against property; the
culpable homicide five. *His* fault is only
against life, and by good fortune he may
escape with a rebuke from the court.

Ralph had been meditating and considering, calmly, earnestly, and at length, in a
way he was not accustomed to consider, and
out here amid evening's impressive silence,
where the brooding peace suggested presences
far enough removed at other times in the
common hubbub of life; and he felt —
what? That he must not give in, or acquiesce in a fiddler's children getting all
that money!

"The higher fitness" was he to call it ?—and
old Gerald himself, who must be near, he was
sure, though he could not gain speech of him
—must disapprove the misapplication of so
many dollars. But how to remedy that ill-
judged will? If Mary Herkimer, it said,
should so far forget herself as to marry the
organist, then the money was to remain accumu-
lating in Jordan's hands for twenty years, and
after that was to be paid to her children,
secured only against the organist by the pro-
vision that in case they died unmarried it

should come to the children of Ralph. And
Mary had a child. But the child might die.
A tremor passed through him at the idea. Or
how would it be, he set himself to consider, if
the child were lost? Children do get lost sometimes, and he raised himself in the canoe to
shake off any oppressiveness that might attach
to the idea. Suppose the child were lost—one
may innocently suppose anything—suppose it
could not be found, and never *were* found.
What then? After a time it would be unrea-
sonable to keep the next in succession out of his
property ; and this next—his blood tingled to
think of it—was his own boy Gerald, a quiet,
gentle little boy, such as strangely sometimes is
given to an unscrupulous father, as if to try how
far he will venture to use the facile tool. If ever
*his* Gerald fell heir to property, Ralph made
sure of being able to dispose of it ; it seemed
to him that it would be like money settled on
his wife, which he could still use, though no
creditor could lay hands on—a cake quite
different from that in the children's proverb,
which one can both eat and have at the same
time.

But at present, to arrange for Mary's child
getting—*lost*, seemed the pressing question.
There would be time enough to influence his
boy's plastic mind afterwards.

The infant's plastic mind need not be taken into account, the infant being only a year old. There were no impressions inscribed on it so far, and it would be some time yet before it acquired any. "Get it away now," he told himself, "and it can do nothing for its own restoration. In a week or two it will have forgotten its mother and there will be no troublesome memories in after life tempting it to suspect and try to unravel a mystery in its fate. Yet how, and through whom, to manage it?" His eyes wandered questioningly over the extent of waters, heaving with regulated swell, suggestive of life and personality and thought; but never an answer came back to him out of the sullen grey. His eye swept the horizon and the distant shore, and at last it rested on the apathetic face of his companion; Still as a mask, and showing not a sign of what might be behind, any more than the swaying tide on which they hung betrayed the mysteries of the pool beneath. The man's long straight hair, and the swarthy skin suggestive of a life apart from civilization, could not but call up the wish that the child could become of these. Wooden, hard, and cold, with his bead-like eyes half closed, were the little one in hands like his it would be as safe as if it were in another planet; thinking such thoughts as it must, in Iroquois, understanding Canadian French, and with only enough English to beg or trade with strangers. Paul he knew as restless, and in some sort a vagabond, attending those who hired him on fishing or hunting expeditions, at times joining the Governor of Hudson's Bay as a canoe-man, on his journeys to Fort William, or wandering on the Ottawa from one Indian settlement to another. If he would only undertake to superintend the fortunes of this inconvenient infant, it would become a waif indeed, and lost beyond restoration.

Ralph sighed with profound relief as the idea passed through his mind. There had been another shadowy suggestion present there all the afternoon, which he had been contemplating as it were with averted eyes, shuddering to consider or reduce to shape, yet refusing to dismiss it, harbouring it as one may an outlaw, whom it would be confusion to acknowledge as a guest. If Paul would undertake the business, the child might live out its life as a squaw among the wigwams of the upper Ottawa, without troubling any one. Exposure to the weather would bronze her to the hue of the other children of the wilderness; and if not, there are few bands now-a-days in which there are not half-breeds, proving that all men are of one blood, and that time and circumstances alone are needed to blend the races into a common stream. How infinitely more satisfactory this would be than any fatal accident which could be devised! Yes! it must be done, and Ralph looked up to his companion and in his most friendly tone said, " Paul."

Instantly the bead-like eyes awoke and turned upon him, sharp and interrogative. The propitiatory modulation had not escaped the delicate ear, bred from infancy to catch and interpret the faintest whisper of the forest—the rustle of a leaf disturbed by passing game, or the stroke of a wing raising eddies in the stagnant air. Since Paul had grown to be a man whiskey and dollars had become the game of his eagerest pursuit, and the mood of the white man he served for the time was the hunting ground where these were to be run down. That something was wanted of him he knew by the extra friendliness of tone. What Englishman having hired him would speak so softly if he did not want something beyond the stipulated services, something of value, and something which he wished to gain cheaply?

" Ouff," was his answer, dubiously interrogative, and altogether non-committal as to whether he would be interested in what was to follow.

"Have you got children?"

"No," with a slight head-shake.

"Would you not like to have one?"

"Papoose come plenty soon."

"Then you have a wife."

"Got squaw;" but still he looked out impassively over the water.

"Would she like to keep a child for me? do you think?—good pay, you know."

"Pay—Ouff?" The words was clearly interrogative now, and the beady eyes returned from their wandering, and settled on the speaker.

"A healthy child twelve months old—would make a lusty squaw. She can make anything of it she likes. No questions will be asked, you know."

"Yours?"

"Not exactly. But I have an interest in the child."

"How much money?"

"Fifty dollars, as soon as she has done the job."

The beady eyes kindled into animation, and the lips grew moist, but the Indian sat motionless as before, and waited in silence for what was to come.

"She will have to *take* the child, you know. It will not be hard for her to get it at this time of year, when the nurse is out of doors with it most of the time; on the steps, at the garden gate, or down the street. She can easily take it away from the nurse, a little slip of a French girl. A strong Indian woman could easily knock her down and run away with the child under her blanket. Only she must not be caught or the child brought back. You must send her to some reservation far away—up West, say—the farther West the better. I will pay as soon as she gets clear off. But you must not mix me up in the thing, mind that! That is why I offer to pay so much for the job."

"Much for job? Ouff. Le Père Théophile—the judge court—prison long time. Ouff!" and he shook his head slowly.

"You must send her where the curé's admonitions will not reach her. Send her to Brantford, or up the Ottawa; you know better than I do where. You can do a good deal with fifty dollars, you know, Paul."

"Ouff. And send 'way my squaw. Fidèle good squaw."

"Chut! Paul, you rascal! You have plenty more sweethearts you know; and they do not marry you so tight as us white men."

Paul grunted. "The Père Théophile very strict. Make squaw confess right up. Poor Fidèle go to prison—all found out. Paul sent to Isle aux Noix—you too, then."

"Stuff, man! No fear of your letting yourself be caught. Send your squaw away at once, before she has time to go near her priest."

"Police?"

"Not much fear of *them*, if you are half sharp. But, let me see. It might not be a bad idea if she changed clothes with some other girl before she started West. One squaw is so like another in white folks' eyes. It might turn pursuit in a wrong direction while she is getting away."

"Ouff," Paul grunted again, but nothing more. The two dusky shadows swung silently on the dim bosom of the waters, whitening now beneath the glimmer of the rising moon.

"See here, Paul," Ralph said at last; "I shall be better than my word after all. Here are ten dollars in hand, for you. Come round to my office as soon as the work is done and your squaw safely off, and I will pay you your fifty dollars. Now land us. We shall take first train to the city. We must not be seen together, so will take different cars. Wait for me in the shadow of the cabstand,

and I will go up town with you and point out the house."

"Ouff," again was the only answer, but as Paul's long arm stretched out to snatch the money, and under a deft stroke or two of the paddle the canoe shot swiftly down stream to the landing, Ralph understood that the bargain was struck.

# CHAPTER V.

## FIDÈLE.

IT was a day or two later, in the early fore-
noon. The air was stagnant, breathlessly
awaiting the thunderstorm whose cumulus
vapour masses were already drifting up from
the distant horizon; though as yet the sun
blazed in cloudless fervour overhead, and the
world lay panting in the intolerable heat.
The very light was sultry, and Mary Selby
had drawn close the blinds, to shut it out
where she lay on a sofa trying to stir the
thick stillness into motion with her fan; but
the air was heavy with heat and she felt too
faint for the exertion.

She was dropping asleep when Lisette
entered with a basket of May apples. They
looked so cool in their green pith-like husks
that she could not refrain from pulling one or
two asunder to reach the blob of fragrant
pulp within, tasting and awakening from her
langour, before she asked where they had

come from. The maid answered that a squaw without was offering them for sale, and the mistress had then to rise and go into an adjoining room to find her purse.

She took the basket in her lap and began to pull open the fruit, separating the small eatable portions from the pod-like rind. " What a feast for Edith! " she said, when she had done ; and she called to Lisette to bring the baby.

Lisette appeared looking hot and troubled. " She had not seen Miss Edith," she said, since she brought the fruit to her mistress—" supposed Cato must have got her. She had been looking for the squaw to give her her money, but could not find her. She thought at first she might be prowling round the house looking for something to steal, but she had looked everywhere now, even in the wood shed and coal cellar, but could not see a sign."

Mary rose to join in the search, running out with the maid to question Cato. Cato was in the far-off corner of the garden, delving with a will. The sultry fervour of the air, stifling to men of another race, was like wine to him, recalling the torrid country of his birth, and he tossed the spadefuls gleefully, perspiring and singing as he worked. He had been there all the morning, and knew nothing of Edith or the vanished squaw; but he threw down his spade at once and joined the searchers. The cook came running from her kitchen to assist, and the little band now quickening each other's alarm ran hither and thither over the small domain, peering under every bush, pulling about melon frames and empty boxes, dropping stones down the well, looking under all the beds in the house and even up the chimney. By-and-by they were out of breath and began to think. Then Lisette was sent for a policeman, and Cato to fetch a cab to carry his mistress in search of her husband, and to the police-station in case he could not be found.

The policeman arrived first with grave importance and a note-book. He questioned Lisette, but being an Irishman while she was French, he soon lost himself amongst her voluble but not very lucid English, emphasized with frequent " *mon Dieux*," and much gesticulation. She was the only one who had seen the squaw, and the last to see the child, but what of that? "Them furreigners were of no account, and nobody could tell what they might be afther intinding to mane;" so he turned to the cook, a countrywoman of his own, and from her got ample satisfaction. It is true she had seen nothing, and only knew

what she had heard Lisette say, but then she
had thought a great deal since; and the
thoughts and the hearsay flowed in a mixed
and copious, if not too coherent stream, which
Paddy could readily follow, it was so much
like the meanderings of his own mind. He
opened his book and proceeded to write it all
down—how she had just finished washing up
her morning dishes, and the pan of water was
in her hands to empty down the sink at that
very moment " whin who should come trapez-
in' into moy kitchen but the gurrl, all brithless
loike, an' hur hair flyin' ivery way at wanst.
An' thinks oi to meself, ' whativer's the mat-
ther wid the omadhaun ? ' An' sorr if I was
to take me boible oath this moment, thim's
the very worrds that passed through me moind
whin I seed hur, an' ye may safely write them
down, for oi'll stand boy thim before all the
judges and juries in the land."

"Oi'll wroite thim down, mum, ye may
depind ; an' be me troth, it's moighty remarkable them worrds are ; an' they do ye credit,
mum, though it's me that says it," answered
the policeman, relaxing the crooks in his
shoulder and elbow, and the frown on his
brow, which were with him the concomitants
of penmanship. He had not in truth the pen
of a ready writer, and it was only by pushing

his tongue into one cheek and closing an eye,
that he was able to construct the letters at all.
That was of little consequence, however; the
notebook was solely for his own private eye,
or rather for the eye of the public, which
could not but respect a policeman who wrote
everything down.

It impressed the cook immensely, and
flattered her too, for never before had she seen
her words put down on paper, and she resolved
in her mind there should be a smoking hot
morsel for this "supayrior" man, whenever
he came round to see her of a winter's afternoon. The man perfectly understood. There
were several kitchens on his beat where he
was wont to visit, and the cook before him
smiled so hospitably that he promised himself
not to forget her.

Cato now arrived with the cab for his
mistress, and the guardian of the peace,
hitherto engrossed with a more important
person, turned to the poor lady to favour her
with a few words at parting.

" You're purfecly right, ma'am," he said,
" to make ivery exurtion. An' if ye call at
the station, ye'll foind the jintlemen there both
poloite an' accommodatin'. An' ye may go wid
an aisy mind, for we'll be havin' your in-
therests under consideration all the same as

if ye was here. An' ye may rest assured that the sthrong arrum of the law will be laid on the aivil doer sooner or later. An' as for the choild, ma'am, oi'm bound to sthop ivery choild of a year old that's carried through my bait; but ye must give me marks, ye see, or they would soon be complainin' of me at head quarthers. Did the choild squint, now, maybe, ma'am, the purty angel? An' it's moighty becomin' some says that same is; an' kinvanient too, whin they gits older, an' can look both ways at wanst. No? Well, no offince, ma'am. Or maybe there was something crooked about wan of its legs, or an arrum, or who knows but there might be something wrong wid its face. A hare lip, now, would be a sure mark, and oi'd arrist the first wan I met. No? Well, no offince, ma'am. Oi cuddn't arrest all the childer I moight meet, ye see, an' bring thim here for you to oidintifee. How many teeth, thin, moight your purty darlin' have, ma'am?— though it's misdoubtin' I am if the law gives me power to open the childher's mouths an' look down their throats. But we'll do our best, ye may depind on that. An' it's wishin' ye a plisant dhroive, ma'am, an' thank ye keoindly," as Mary, driven desperate by his gabble, pushed a dollar into his hand and hurried to her cab.

In this way "the law's delays" left the coast clear for the escape of the kidnapper. It was an hour or two before the police throughout the city became aware that a squaw had run away with an infant, and by the time they had begun to be on the alert, the thief had made good her retreat. Wrapped in her bright blue blanket and broad-leafed straw hat, she passed swiftly along, as might any of her fellows who hawk their beadwork and like wares about the streets. A lump of fat, rubbed in the juice of some narcotic herb, pushed into the little mouth had stilled the child's cries and made it sleep as though in its nurse's arms—evidence of the practical wisdom of the wilderness still lingering among its erewhile people, as yet but partially elevated to our higher plane of life. Our women may become doctors of divinity, law, or physic ; they can play the piano, or stand in the front rank of culture ; but can they handle a baby like the artless daughters of the North-West, whose charges, packed in moss and fur, strapped upon a board and suspended from a branch, sway gently in the breeze, watching and growing silently, like the plants, for hours together, with never a cry to disturb the resting sire or the laborious mother? In the march of improvement some useful knowledge has been dropped by the way, and there are regrettable losses to set off against the manifest gains.

The thunder which had been threatening all the morning began to rumble, the sky darkened, and soon the rain came down in torrents. The ferry-boat between Lachine and Caughnawaga had whistled, and was throwing loose from the wharf, when a squaw —it was Fidèle, Paul's squaw, of course—rain-soaked and draggled, leaped on board. She squatted on the deck beside the three or four others who were the only passengers, cowering over the bundle under her blanket, but not uncovering its face as did the mothers near her.

"She has stolen something," the purser observed to the mate, "and is passing it off for a child. She don't behave to it as the others do. If there is a constable on the pier, I'll give her in charge. But there won't be in this heavy rain, and there would be a row if we attempted to stop her. Best take no notice, I guess; 'taint no business of ours."

On reaching the pier, Fidèle was the first to land and flit away through the village. "I told you so," said the purser, looking wise. "You just see if we don't hear more about that one. Blue blanket, with a tear in one corner; straw hat—brim badly broken; face,

like they all have—broad and brown as a
butternut ; red cheeks—must be young—and
real spry on the pins. Guess I'd know her
again—know the clothes, any way. Injuns
are as like one another as copper cents."

Fidèle reached a cabin in the outskirts, of
square logs, whitewashed, one window and a
door, with a "lean-to" addition of boards in
the rear, where the cooking·stove stood in the
warm weather. Entering, she found her sister
Thérèse awaiting her, who with very few
words proceeded to strip off her own brightly
printed cotton gown. Fidèle carried the child
into the room behind, and returning, removed
her blanket and dripping headgear.

"Ouff," said Thérèse, undoing the gay
handkerchief from her head and picking up
the hat in evident disgust. "No good."

There was a small silver cross hanging from
her neck by a black riband, to which Fidèle
stretched out her hand expecting it to be taken
off likewise. But no. Thérèse drew back
with a head-shake, explaining that that belonged to the ladies of the Convent school,
adding, that it was bad enough to give up the
smart frock and kerchief in exchange for such
a hat and a damp blanket. Fidèle reminded
her of the new ones she was to receive from
Paul, after she had worn the blanket for a

week, and again snatched at the nuns' silver badge of merit. Thérèse caught the hand and bit it. Fidèle screamed, and a battle was imminent, when Paul's growl from the back room, threatening violence, restored calm, and Thérèse sulkily took up the blanket and drew it over her head. Presently, Paul looked out to bid her begone, and Thérëse, through the open door, saw enough to silence remonstrance, and send her trembling away.

Paul entered as Thérèse went out, and stood before his squaw. He spoke in Iroquois, briefly, and in the conclusive tone which admits neither of question nor reply. Another, Messieurs the Benedicts, of those natural gifts dropped by the way in the march of improvement. The squaw never "speaks back," but the "last word" belongs of right to every self-respecting Christian woman, and she takes it. Ask the ladies!

"To work at once," was the purport of Paul's orders, "then sweep up. Put on your sister's gown, and that black blanket over all. Go out by the back, into the bush. Hide in the old roothouse by the corner of the clearing till sundown; then away, across the reservation. Take care you are not seen. Travel all night, going west. Stay in the woods to-morrow till dusk. Travel your

quickest till you reach Ogdensburg. Cross
the river there, and go west to Brantford, taking your own time. Go to your brother, and
tell him to expect me next winter." And so
saying, he went out by the front of the house,
locking the door behind him.

Fidèle set her teeth and proceeded to obey.
It was a repulsive sight which she beheld on
entering the inner room, and the work set her
to do was horrible. A board or two of the
flooring had been pulled up, and there was a
sack filled with the earth brought up through
the opening. The hole was a foot or two
deep, and it was shaped like a grave. Paul
must have been terribly in earnest to have
it rightly done, seeing he had dug it himself.
There was a box—a soap-box seemingly, from
the village store—hammer and nails, a bundle
of withered grass, and the baby asleep lying
on it. The sight of the baby must have been
too much for Paul, for part of an old buffalo
robe had been thrown over it. He had
his design fixed and firm, but having also a
squaw why should he likewise discompose
himself? Civilization had at least eaten so far
into his nature that to extinguish a helpless
and unresisting life was no longer delightful
enough to compensate the risk—and he had
the squaw.

Fidèle sat down on the ground with the poor little thing in her lap. How peacefully it slept! Was it angels whispering in those little ears which made it smile in its sleep, as the ladies of the Convent had said? Could viewless spirits be hovering around, seeing and noting all that passed? Involuntarily she looked over her shoulder expecting almost to behold a presence. Then she shook herself and snorted. Why should she call up shadowy fears to make harder for herself the work she had to do? If she failed to do it she knew full surely the terrors would be all too real— bruises, wounds, possibly death by violence; assuredly violence in any less degree.

The child lay sleeping on her lap, so fair and soft of skin, rounded and dainty in every joint. She could not but recall the picture in the church, of the Holy Mother with her ever Blessed Son, high up above the altar, amid the star-like twinkling of the tapers and the cloudy incense ascending before it in solemn fragrance, while holy nuns and innocent choristers sang hymns of adoration; and all she had learned to think of blessedness beyond the grave, attainable only by more than common goodness, was that it would be like that. The little rings of hair that framed the face were bright and shining like burnished gold, a glory like the gilded halos about the heads in that sacred picture; and the long eyelashes laid peacefully upon the reddening cheeks, like clouds at daybreak, promising so enhanced a brightness at the awakening. Fidèle laid her fingers on the little neck. How dark and evil they looked upon its creamy whiteness! How could she ever grasp it hard and cruelly, till the heaving bosom grew convulsed to bursting at the interrupted breath, and the sweet face grew black and distorted in fruitless gaspings? Her fingers lay more heavily as she thought, and the slight pressure disturbed the sleeper. The plump round shoulder and cheek were drawn together as if tickling were the subject of her dreams; the lips parted in a smile, the eyes unclosed, and the child awoke with a low and merry laugh. She looked so fearless and trustful out of her blue eyes and crowed so gleefully, caressing with her own tiny palms the dusky fingers so near her throat, and with such fell intent, that surely a fiend must have abandoned the thought of doing her harm. And Fidèle was no fiend at all. Ignorance and a narrow horizon had left her sympathies to slumber, but, so far as she could see or know, she was true and good. To serve her man had seemed the chief if not the only end of her being, and she had done it

blindly hitherto ; but it appeared to her now
that to do this thing was more than she ought,
or could.

The little hands were stretched up now to
her face and the lips strained up to kiss her,
and the clear blue light of the eyes penetrated
the blackness of her own with a cooling purify-
ing influence which made evil intent like a
shadow slink away. She stooped and pressed
the little pink lips to her own, and to her forehead and to her breast, and then with a big
breath of resolution she got up and set the
little one down in a corner while she fulfilled
in seeming the orders she had received. She
took the dried grass and laid it in the box
which she then closed and placed in the bottom
of the little grave. The grave she then filled up
with earth from the sack, tramping it down
tightly, and making the top level with the ad-
jacent soil, and strewing what earth was left
in the rain pools outside the house. She then
nailed down the flooring as before, and swept
the house, making it appear again as it had
always been. No one could now suspect that
there was a grave beneath his feet, nor could
Paul that that grave was empty. Then con-
cealing the child under her blanket she stole
into the bush as she had been instructed
to do, an instance of how the scrupulously

obedient wife, even while obeying, may contrive to effect the exact opposite of her instructions; and showing, perhaps, that the equality and sympathy of the civilized home may secure a man the fulfilment of his wishes no less, at least, than the despotism of the barbarian plan.

In the twilight Fidèle left her place of concealment and stole away under the dripping trees. The storm was over, and as the light died out of the heavens the stars came twinkling forth, awaiting the rising moon. It was a long and toilsome tramp across the reservation, through wet and tangled herbage, with many a slough and flooded brook, for she had been bidden to avoid observation and dared not avail herself of such paths and rude bridges as suffice the Indians on their own domain. At length when night had fully come, and home-going stragglers were no longer likely to be met, she reached a country road. The march of the stars pointed her way and further she knew not, for she had never been there before. She hurried along clasping her burden, which grew heavier as she went, for she had been travelling for hours. It was late and she had spent a long and a busy day, a day of hard work and much excitement. The child grew heavier, and as her own strength grew less, she clasped it the more tightly. Since she had saved the little one's life, something of a mother's feeling for it had stolen into her heart. It seemed dependent on her, and her very own ; and were not the tiny fingers even then spreading themselves against her breast to gather warmth? The night seemed very long, and yet she feared to stop and rest. A pursuer might be on her track even now to seize her for child-stealing. And the child in her arms! She could not but be taken and punished, and the child given back. And even when her punishment was over, and she let out of jail, there would still be Paul to reckon with. And what might *he* not do? Her heart died within her at the thought, her limbs grew feeble, and the child heavier than lead. She staggered along looking behind her and before, but all was still, no one to be seen. And now she was approaching a village. The moonlight glittered on the tin belfry of the church, and there were houses, low-browed *habitant* houses, with deep projecting eaves and great black shadows lurking under the stoops and porches. Not a soul was stirring, but from those coverts of obscurity what or who might not rush forth on her as she went by? The law in some mysterious way might be lying in wait for her among the dusky

6—2

shadows, or Paul himself might be in hiding to watch her pass, and see that he was obeyed. It would be bad for her if she were to meet him now, and bad for the child as well. She stopped, faltering as she thought of it, unable to go on. Ah! there stood one small house at a forking of the road, where one branch ran uphill through well-fenced woods, surrounding a mansion, doubtless, for the moonlight glistened on the tin of the roof; and the other branch ran downward to the village and the church, and there was a broad river beyond, with perhaps no bridge, and she might have to wait for morning to be ferried across. There might be a magistrate in the mansion, she would avoid that, and down in the village the child might be seen. No! she dared not carry it in either direction, but here in the corner of the ways stood the little *habitant* house, a good half-mile from both. Yet there was no light visible in the window; the house might be uninhabited; not a dog or pig was to be seen around. But then it was late. The voiceless stars and the silent sailing moon were whitening the slumbering world with dim and hazy dreams. Nothing was awake or moving but the vagrant breeze which rustled drowsily among the poplar leaves; and—yes, that decided her—the loose casement of the one

window in the roof swaying back and forth
against the flapping curtains within. There
must be people in the house, people asleep,
who would not awake till she had time to escape. She stepped on the little porch, laid
down her burden, knocked, and fled into a
neighbouring bank of shadow, where her
dark blanketed figure was swallowed up in
the gloom and she could wait and watch.
Her moccasined feet made no sound, but the
knock awoke a dog within. The dog barked,
and presently a head looked out of the open
casement. The baby, uncovered to the night
air and laid on the hard boards, began to cry,
and the head—it was a woman's and a
mother's—recognized the voice of a *bébé*. The
door was opened, the woman came out and
took up the child.

"Holy Madaleine!—it is a child! And
whose? Another, when there are already
six, and the loaf so small, and the *sous* so
hard to come by!"

Fidèle saw, and she may have heard; but
she could not understand or enter into the
white woman's troubled feelings. *Sous* scarce
and loaves small were just as she knew them,
when she knew them at all, which was not
always. At least it was better, both for herself and the child, that it should not be with

*her.* She waited till the woman had carried it indoors, and then, like a wandering shadow, she went her way, westward, with the stars and moon. Her friends, her home, her man, were all behind her, and she must not return to them. She must go forward and westward to Upper Canada, a wanderer and alone, with nothing but the stolid patience of her unawakened mind to bear her up. But at least her hands were untainted with the stain of blood, and she could look forward to the long dark winter nights and their howling winds without fear. There would be no voices in them to make her tremble, no cry of a murdered child—no image in the darkness of gasping lips and eyes rolled back in the death-struggle. She could sleep in peace and still ask God and His saints to shelter her.

# CHAPTER VI.

## THE MISSES STANLEY.

The Misses Stanley were sitting up far into the night. They had been prostrated in the morning by the sultry oppression of the coming storm. Later, when it burst, and the blackened sky grew ablaze with lightning, and the very earth was trembling at the deafening thunder-claps, they fled to the cellar, closing and bolting the door, in that unreasoning panic which seizes even very sensible people when the heavens begin to utter their terrible voices; and there they gasped, and sighed, and panted, and listened, forgetting even the headache which a while before had nailed their heads to the pillow. "Ah!" they would whisper to each other, "did you hear that?—and that?—One of the chimneys has surely been struck! Can that be the rattle of the falling bricks? Is the roof coming down, do you think? Are we safe here?" and they caught each other's

hands and pressed them tightly, and leaned
against the door with all their might, to keep
it shut against the danger.

"Do you hear that hissing? Has the house
taken fire? Do you smell smoke?" It was
only the first heavy downpour of the rain
upon the resounding tin roof. The steady
continuance of the monotone assured them of
that in time, as the thunder grew intermittent
and less loud. Even the hissing of the rain
grew faint after a while, and there came a
breath of cooler air down even into the
locked-up cellar.

The terror was past, and they crept out
of their hole again into the light, like the
mice and the spiders and other timid folk.
The storm was over and they were happy and
safe. They had been able to eat no breakfast;
dinner had been standing on the table cooling
and getting spoiled while they were trembling
in the cellar. So they had tea, and partook
of it with relish. The air was purified by
the storm; it was reviving to breathe it, and
the world, seen through the open windows,
though wet, was brightened and refreshed by
the rain, like a young girl fresh from the
luxury of a good cry.

It was sweet to be alive now, and drink in
the scented air, so crisp and fresh, yet without

a suspicion of cold ; and a while since life had been a burden. The ladies sat and breathed, and sighed, and toyed with existence, and spoke softly to one another, and were silent; and evening wore on and night came, and still it was too pleasant to move. Their lamp was lighted—a dim one, with no garish gleam to disturb enjoyment within, or lure the flapping night-moths and beetles from without—and feeling hungry they thought they would have supper, a most unusual thing. It was but strawberries and cakes with lemonade and cold tea, but for them it was a carouse ; they sat picking and sipping for very long, forgetful of time, and most other things, and bathed by gentle stirrings of the soothing air, restful and in soft shadow, while in the moonlit garden without, the white radiance was reflected and broken into a hundred glittering sparkles from every dripping leaf.

"I declare," said the younger sister, "midnight is decidedly the most enjoyable part of the day, at this time of year."

"It is long past midnight, Matilda," her sister answered, "I am afraid to look what hour of the morning it must be."

"Morning? To-morrow morning? This is to-morrow then! I like it ; and if we go to

bed it will be to-day when we get up again.
I prefer to-morrow myself. Let's sit up all
night, Tookey dear, and remain in the future
' till daylight does appear,' and turns it into
to-day again. Commonplace affair that sun,
compared to the moon, and disagreeably hot
at this season, besides. I envy the owls, and
mice, and bats, and things, coming out at
night and sleeping all day. *I* can't sleep in the
daytime."

"The more need to go to bed at night.
Come, Tilly!—or how shall we get up in
the morning? Late rising puts everything
out of joint for all day, and bothers the poor
servants sadly."

" Bother the servants ! By all means, say I.
' Never do to-morrow what should be done
to-day.' You know that is a proverb! And
this is to-morrow. It was you who said so ;
so let us sit still. I think I have proved
my case."

" Pshaw, Matilda ! don't be childish. And
the downstairs windows still to shut up !
Bring the light, dear. We'll make the round,
and see that all is fast."

It was a nightly procession in which these
two ladies walked through all the rooms on
the ground floor. Miss Penelope the elder—
called Tookey for short by her sister—went

first, trying the locked doors, closing and bolting the windows, while Matilda with a candle held aloft, kept close beside her. It fluttered her heart to go into an empty room after dark, and it caught her breath to remain alone in the drawing-room while her sister made the rounds, so she accompanied her close, always within touching distance, and ready to scream should occasion arise. Last of all they closed the drawing-room windows, and barred the heavy inside shutters, provided with bells, so that no housebreaker should be able to enter without ringing ; and then with their candlesticks in their hands, having extinguished the lamp, they stood taking a last look, as it were, on the scene of their waking existence, before wending upstairs to sleep and forgetfulness, when——

Bang ! The sound seemed deafening, coming as it did so unexpectedly, in the night stillness, with all the world slumbering save themselves. Again ! Not so loud this time, it seemed, with the ear already attentive. It was a knock at the hall door. And now the bell was rung, a jangling peal resounding through the house, and under cover of the uproar there was a crunching on the gravel as of hasty steps.

The sisters looked at one another with

parted lips, and eyes that sought help and counsel and assurance each in the other's. Matilda assuredly had neither strength nor wisdom for their joint support, but her need was so great and she looked with such fervent trustfulness at her sister, that Penelope felt she must brace herself up and take courage for both, though her heart was faint within her. She was the object of a faith which supported by its helpless reliance, and stimulated her to effort that it might not prove misplaced. So strength ere now has been bred of double weakness, though in this case it was put forth but falteringly at first.

There was a shuffling now and a whispering in the lobby. Penelope held the door handle and listened. Matilda threw her weight against the door, expecting it would be burst open; but it was not, and thus they stood breathlessly awaiting some unspecified terror which did not arrive, till doubt grew too painful, and Penelope in very desperation flung wide the door. Three pale faces were disclosed blinking at the gleam of the ladies' candles, and Matilda screamed. An answering scream was raised by the three pale faces startled by the sudden flash of light in the darkened passage, and already prepared to be frightened by anything which might happen.

" How very foolish!" said Miss Penelope,
who, having wrought herself up to do battle
of some kind, had her nerves better in
hand. "Do you not see it is the servants?
Awakened by the noise, they have come
downstairs, and seeing light in here at such
an hour, supposed it was a thief. Now we
must see who is at the front door."

" No, Penelope! I implore you, do not!"

" Oh, ma'am," said the cook, " if anything
happens to *you* what will become of *us* ?" and
the other maids looked deprecating in con-
cert, while even Miss Matilda ejaculated,
" What, indeed ?"

" We cannot stand here all night! And we
could not go to bed with burglars perhaps waiting on the doorstep till we are asleep."

" Think, Penelope, if they should burst in
when we unbar the door!"

" They had better not. Is there not my
father's gun?" and so saying she stepped on
a chair to reach down that redoubtable
weapon from where it rested on two brass
hooks, high up over the fireplace in the hall.
There it had rested ever since the decease
of the late lamented Deputy Assistant Com-
missary General—called General for short, or
perhaps for honour—the parent of the Misses
Stanley.

"Oh, Tookey! don't!" cried Miss Matilda. "It might go off and hurt some one," and the maids drew up their shoulders to their ears, and looked apprehensive in chorus.

"Nonsense!" answered Miss Stanley severely. "Do you not see I am pointing it to the ceiling?"

"One never knows, such strange things happen with guns. The barrels burst, they say, or else they go off, and shoot the people they have no business to touch, and let others escape who really ought to have been hit. Remember how poor Major Hopkins' gun went off, nobody knew how, and killed papa's spaniel, and let the duck fly away. I shall never forget how cross poor papa was when he came home, and he never asked Major Hopkins to come again." And Miss Matilda looked regretful, as does the Historic Muse when she registers the might-have-beens. "Pray point the muzzle up the chimney, dear; it is safer."

Penelope, with a disdainful shrug, moved to the door, raised her firearm to her shoulder, and motioned the maids to undo the fastenings and open. They obeyed, and as the door flew back there entered a puff of wind which blew out the candles and made everybody scream—everybody except Miss Stanley. She, like a hero, stood to her gun, and pulled the trigger—she pulled it frequently, in fact, but as the piece was not loaded, that made no difference. Indeed, it was much better, her timid companions were saved the dreadful bang, while she herself had the heroic feeling of having shot a gang of burglars; that is, she would have shot them if her gun had been loaded, and they had been there to be shot. But they were not, fortunately for themselves. There was no one there at all. The band of affrighted females came slowly to realize the fact, as their panic subsided, and they re-lit the candles. "But who," they began to inquire, "could it be, who had knocked so loudly and rung the bell?" As their tremors abated they ventured out upon the verandah, which ran round the house, to reconnoitre. There was no one there, and again they grew uneasy. The visitant must have concealed himself in the shrubbery, and if so, he must certainly be evil-disposed. Miss Stanley took up her gun again; she had no misgiving about handling it now, and it looked as formidable as ever, for of course the man in the shrubbery could not know that it was unloaded, and she made sure he would not put its being so to the test.

"Here is a large parcel, ma'am!" cried the parlour-maid, "shall I bring it in? It is covered with old matting and tied with a shoe-string."

"Take care, Rhoda!" said Matilda. "Let us look at it first. I have heard of thieves tying themselves up in parcels in order to be taken into the houses they intended to rob. Perhaps you had better fire your gun into this, Penelope; I have known that to be done in a story with the best effects."

Miss Penelope came to look. "I think we may take this one in, Tilly, without fear. If it contains a man he cannot be very big. See! I can lift the bundle myself. Bring it in, Rhoda; we will examine it in the dining-room."

"It must be living, ma'am! I see it moving. Will it bite?" and she took it up suspiciously and with precaution.

A cry, small and plaintive, was now heard. "Do you hear that?" said Miss Matilda. "mewing — I think. Can anybody have brought us a cat and kittens? A practical joke I suppose they think it. Yet I like kittens,—soft little balls of fluff and fun," she went on, putting on her gloves at the same time, "but strange cats may bite or scratch. Very impertinent, was it not, of the senders? They mean, I suppose, that we are old maids. Well! If we are, at least it is

from choice, and I venture to say we are
more comfortably situated than the husband
or wife of this impertinent."

"Tush! sister," said Penelope, glancing to
the servants standing at the lower end of the
table and full of curiosity. "Have you a
penknife? Quick! No cat ever mewed like
that."

And now indeed it was a lusty cry, distinctly
human and articulating mamma. The string
was cut, the wrappings were kicked away by
the struggling contents of the parcel, and a
good-sized, healthy infant, well nourished,
well clad, flushing red in the opening
paroxysm of a big cry on waking, was disclosed to view.

"A little child!" cried Miss Matilda in
transports.

"What a frightful din!" said Miss Stanley,
putting her fingers in her ears. "To think
that anything so small should make so much
noise! What ever shall we do with it?"

"Give it some milk, of course; bathe it,
put it to bed. That is what they always do
with babies, I believe. Cook! get hot water
at once—and a large basin—and some milk—
and—and—everything else that is necessary.
Quick! you others, and help her," she added,
observing the lingering steps of the maids,

yawning now, and utterly disgusted and wishing themselves back in bed, though a moment ago they had been all wakefulness and interest.

It was curious to see how Matilda took the lead, now that her sympathies were appealed to, while her practical sister, the mistress and manager of the establishment, stood aside bewildered and confused. She took the child in her arms and walked up and down, dandling it, singing, and purring forth floods of baby talk, till the little one stopped short in the middle of its lament to look at her, and ascertain who this voluble person might be. Then, finding she could make out nothing by her scrutiny, she prepared to resume with augmented vigour, but Matilda would not have it. She sat down with the doubter in her lap, bent over it, and made a bower for it with her curls, crooning more volubly than ever, and tickling it with the ringlet points, till the astonished infant grew confused, forgot that it had intended to scream, and presently was smiling and crowing and pulling the ringlets like bell-ropes.

Miss Matilda's ringlets were perhaps her most noticeable feature—long, waving, twining masses of falling hair; giving her face a pensive and romantic expression which has long ceased to be fashionable, though it once was greatly admired, as was also the poetry of Moore and Mrs. Hemans about the same time. In her youth, and that was not so many years before, an officer in Montreal—it was there the family lived then—had told her she looked like a muse, and not long after he was ordered away to the Crimean war. Her own father was ordered there too, but he said he owed a higher duty to his motherless daughters than to leave them, and he thought he owed it to his own ease not to let himself be sent ranging over Asia Minor, Syria, and Egypt, in search of transport mules and donkeys, and so he left the Service. He lingered in Montreal after the troops were withdrawn; but soon that community of busy traders grew insupportable in the absence of his fellow-loungers; he bought a farm near Saint Euphrase, and there established himself, carrying his daughters with him. He had already, as he told them, sacrificed his prospects of advancement to their need of a protector, and now it was for them to yield the social comforts of town life, bury themselves in the country, and with grateful assiduity make his home as comfortable, and his rheumatism as little intolerable as possible. After the fall of Sebastopol the troops returned to Canada,

and " General " Stanley was able from time
to time to relieve the monotony of his retirement with the society of old friends; but the
officer who had called Matilda a muse never
re-appeared, and no other gentleman since
had said anything half as nice. So Matilda
cherished her ringlets and her recollections—
not very painful ones—and lived tranquilly
on, with no event to mark the flight of years,
till the death of her father, which took place
some three or four years before the time I
write of. After that the sisters lived on as
before, only more retiredly still. Miss Penelope developed considerable business faculty
in managing their affairs, and overlooking
Jean Bruneau, the factotum on the farm ; and
dropped some of the feminine helplessnesses
of her youth, though she was still as much in
terror of thunder, burglars, fire and snakes as
ever. Matilda having less need to exert her
powers, continued the same ringletted damsel
she had always been. She busied herself with
her flowers and her birds, a little music not
too difficult or new, a little poetry and fiction,
and a good deal of kindness when the need
for it was made plain to her. Her youth was
passing or had passed into middle life, but the
current of her days had been so even that
she had not observed their flight. She had

had no cares, and her heart slept peacefully, for it had never been awakened. Captain Lorrimer may have called her a muse, and Major Hopkins may have looked in her eyes, but these things had never been carried to a disturbing length; just enough to afford a little pensive self-consciousness, when she read of deserted maids, or Love's young dream, and make her fancy that she understood it all, and ejaculate that "it was so true." Then she would look up and shake her curls with a quite comfortable sigh, and her prosaic sister would watch her admiringly, and wonder where the men's eyes could have been that she was still unmarried. Perhaps it was well for her that she was so. Perhaps it would be well, at least it would be comfortable, for many of us if our hearts would sleep through life, and leave digestion to do its work in peace. How sweet and enjoyable to lead untroubled lives, free from the ecstasies alike of joy and woe, as do the flowers, as did this "muse"—this "grass of Parnassus"—basking in summer suns and drinking dews, without ambition or desire or strife.

But this is wandering. We left Miss Penelope desirous of getting to bed; and Miss Matilda engrossed in her new plaything.

"I shall certainly keep it, Penelope! The

very thing of all others I should have liked
best to have."

"Is not that rather an odd thing to say?"

"That I am charmed to have found a living
doll?—I think it is quite natural. *You* are
too sensible, of course, but for other people
—for me—it seems the most natural thing in
the world. You know I always doted on dolls,
especially when they could wink their eyes.
This one can do that, and lots of other things
besides. It will be delightful. And to think
how I have been mourning the loss of my lame
canary these last few days! You would not
believe the tears I have shed every time I have
looked at the empty cage, and how lonely I have
felt; and here, in the middle of the night, just
when we are going to bed, arrives this little
pet! Is it not opportune? If I had awakened in
the night, I might have thought of poor dicky,
and then I should certainly have cried. Now
I shall take this sweet little image with me, and
if I awake, it will be to think how I can make
up to it the loss of its mother; though indeed
the mother who could find it in her breast to
cast her off in this disgraceful way can be no
loss."

# CHAPTER VII.

## THE DESOLATE MOTHER.

IT was three months later. The Selbys' shrubbery had changed from the vigorous greens of summer to russet, paling here into sulphur yellow, there deepening to orange and crimson which outshone the less vivid tints of the early chrysanthemums. The autumn flowers, nipped by early frosts, lay black and ragged on their erewhile brilliant beds. The sun was warm and the air sweet with the breath of leaves falling softly in their brightness, one by one, peaceful, beautiful, fragrant, like the ending of a well-spent life.

In the parlour the windows were open; and a fire burning in the grate to temper the air in shady corners proclaimed the fall of the year.

Stretched on a sofa, thin and wan, with hair pushed back—hair which three months before had been soft and glossy and of the loveliest

brown, now dry, rusty, grizzled, banded with
locks of grey, and mixed all through with
threads of shining white—her fingers shrunk
and bloodless, clasping a baby's bells and
coral, and her dim eyes wet with silent tears,
lay the desolate mother mourning for her
child. She had been very ill, and bodily
weakness, unable to suffer more, was the one
consoler as yet to mitigate her grief, by be-
numbing the capacity for pain. Her George
had mingled tears with hers, tears drawn as
much by the sight of what she suffered as by
its cause. He had tended and watched her
with more than a woman's tenderness, but
after all he was a man, with his day's work to
perform whatever might befall, and the doing
it supported him by bringing distraction and
thereby rest. True, it jarred miserably on
the overwrought nerves to keep up the routine
of music lessons, to watch the " fingering " of
inattentive pupils and have his senses pierced
by their frequent discords ; but it was easier
to find endurance for these physical ills than
for the heartstrain he had felt at home. The
patience and fatigue of the outdoor toil
brought the calmness he needed so much in
the presence of his stricken wife.

For her there was no break or respite to the
rush of black and miserable thought. If the

child had died she could have borne it. It would
have been grief, but grief of the common
kind, and for which there is consolation in
the pious certainties of another life. It would
have been agony to part with her treasure,
but agony with a hope. In time she would
have learned to bear the bereavement with
sorrowful patience and resignation—to think
of her blossom snatched away, rather as one
transplanted and someday to be recovered in
brighter bloom, growing in immortal gardens;
just as she looked on the other—brother of
the lost one, born since her loss, and which
had never seen the light. Oh, if she could but
have thought of the two as with each other!
But even the consolations of faith were denied
her. The child had vanished utterly, and she
was left to wonder and surmise whither it
might have been carried. Surely if it had
died there would have been found some sign
or vestige, and then her mother's heart would
have been at rest. She would have wept and
there would have been an end. She could have
rested her thoughts on the armies of the Holy
Innocents, and in her dreams a cherub face
would have come to her with shining wings,
whispering hope and consolation. But even
this saddened peace was not for her. She
would not entertain the thought that her

baby was dead; it was away somewhere—
where, oh where?—and perhaps it needed
her, and was crying for her, and she could
not come to it; and a restlessness seized her,
a low dull fever of impotent longing, and
kept her pacing the chamber to and fro, till
exhaustion numbed her senses and she fell
asleep. But oh, what sleep! It was more
miserable than waking. Fancy gave shape
to her yearnings, and dreams revived their
wretchedness into more tangible shape. The
baby's cry, as if in pain, rang through them
all, and sometimes she could see the arms
stretched out to her, but never the face. A
shadow undefined came in between, and bore
her darling away into darkness. Sometimes
her feet would be heavy as lead, and scarcely
could she drag herself after, while the shadow
fled out of sight, and the cries came to her fit-
fully, and far away, borne on the wind. At
other times she would be able to pursue, but
that brought little comfort. The shadow still
fled before her, and ah, by what dreary
ways! Sometimes it would be dark, and yet
she could see them speeding on before; across
a raging river, where the waters tossed and
tumbled about her, lifting her from her feet,
or overwhelming her in their depths; but still
she hurried on and clambered up the slippery

rocks on the further shore, and up and up where there was no foothold, and she felt herself falling through depths and catching and clinging with her hands and drawing herself upward and up and up among curling mists to dreary deserts far above the clouds. And still the shadow sped on before, and she pursued across the sandy wastes, where horrid reptiles hissed at her as she went by, and clouds of dust arose and came between, obscuring and impeding the way. And still she would pursue and seem to be overtaking. The child's cry would become quite close, and she would see the very dimples at the finger joints and the streaming hair, and she would stretch her hand to lay it on the form, and her hand would pass through it like a shadow and she would awake. It was all a dream, her darling was gone from her and she was desolate.

On the day of the theft she had driven about the town in search of her husband, sometimes hearing of him but never meeting ; and then she had gone to the police station herself, breathless with anxiety and haste, and there they were so mechanical and full of formalities, and heard her story with so aggravating an official calm that it wellnigh drove her mad. The person she addressed on entering was sweltering on two chairs, without coat or collar, and his boots pulled off. Before he would listen to a lady he felt it due to himself to rectify his appearance. The boots were tight and could not be quickly stepped into; the coat was on a nail in another part of the office. Then the book of complants had to be found, and a pen, and so many flies had drowned themselves in the ink that the stand must be refilled, and Mary stood wringing her hands and swaying back and forth in agonized impatience.

"Calm yourself, madame," he said, while he dipped in the ink his pen, and then removed first a dead fly from the point, and next a hair. "I shall now take down your complaints," and he bent over his book, extending his left elbow and bending his head towards it, with the eyes squinting across the page he was about to illustrate with his caligraphy, while with an expert turn of the wrist he made a preliminary flourish in waiting for this member of the public to begin stating her grievance; "but stay one moment, madame; I believe I have mislaid my glasses;" and he started up and laid his hand upon each of his pockets in turn. "No! I believe I must have lef dem in ze ozer desk beside ze journaux."

"Oh man! man!" cried Mary in desperation, "while you are putting off time my baby is being carried further and further away; and we know not where she may be or what they are doing to her!"

"Be tranquillisée madame! Ze occurrence —is of frequent—how you say?—occurrence. Zere are tree—five!" and he held up his fingers to show the number—"infants vich make disappearance all ze days, and zey all turn zemselves up again before to-morrow. Ze leetle tings march in ze streets voisines, and know not ze retour. Ze police arrest, and bring here; and voilà!—l'enfant perdu ees on return to ze famille." At this point the spectacles were discovered, and the speaker returned to his book.

"My baby *could* not run away. She cannot walk yet." Mary answered. "My baby has been carried off, and you are wasting precious time in talk."

"Ze publique ees so déraisonnable! And me. Behold me!"—and he spread out all his fingers and shrugged his shoulders in philosophic and forbearing remonstrance— "I attend madame's informations."

The "informations" were given, recorded and commented on, and the slow machinery of justice set in motion at last, and the

distracted mother turned away to the grey
nunnery where foundlings are received and
cared for.  There she left a description of her
child, and begged that if any one resembling
hers were presented, she might at once be
informed.  Then she went home.  What to
her was the thunder storm and lashing rain?
A wilder tempest of doubt raged in her own
aching heart.  Her husband had arrived
before her, and in tears on his shoulder she
found the first momentary easement since her
trouble began.  The world was so hard and
callous, so busy, every one with his own
affairs; people accepted her desolation so
calmly, told her not to fret, that the child would
soon be found.  She could not have believed
the atrocious selfishness of mankind if she
had not seen it.  The street children,
playing after the rain, were as gleeful as ever,
without a thought of her distress; losing their
balls across the fence and coming over after
them— breaking in on her very inclosure,
sacred to miserable anxiety, as if nothing
were the matter.  Her own servants were no
better, they were going on with their cooking
and their housework just as usual.  There
was the dinner bell!  Who could think of
dinner on a day like this?  And yet George
—and she could not but own that George had

proper feeling, and was as anxious and distressed as a *man* well could be—even George seemed to have bodily appetite. He was not cannibal enough to dine, but he did eat a slice of beef, and drink a tumbler of wine and water. It seemed incomprehensible to her, somehow, that even the round heavens should revolve as usual. But they did. It was growing dark just the same as if nothing had befallen her baby, and the long still night was before her. There were hours and hours to wait before another day would arise, with its possibilities of news or restoration, and how was she to spend them? She could not sit still, far less lie down. She wondered about the house hour after hour, and three several times her husband took a cab to the police head-quarters in vain. There was no news.

The morrow brought no change; but weariness stilled the restlessness of her misery. She could not eat or drink or sleep, or even wander to and fro; she could but wait, seated in the porch and watching the gate for coming news—for news which did not come. The chief of police appeared, and questioned Lisette and went again. Another day, and Lisette was sent for to see Indians taken upon suspicion, and in the evening she returned having identified one. But still there was no news of the child. The squaw arrested declared she knew nothing of it, had not taken it, had not been in the city that day.

And now Mary's strength gave way. She fainted, and when revived it was found that she was dangerously ill; and through long weeks her life trembled on the verge of dissolution, flickering and waning till it seemed scarce possible the spark should not go out. And then, too weak to suffer, she began to mend, and in the vacuity of utter exhaustion, her mind obtained that rest which no doubt saved her reason, sparing her the weary waitings on for news which never came. In her illness a son was born—was born and died—but only in her convalescence did she become aware of her loss. That was a grief, but it was grief of the more ordinary kind, and one to which the Church's consolations effectively minister. The little one's earthly sojourn was accomplished; it needed her care no longer, and the hopes of religion were a soothing balm to mingle with her tears. But the other?— She was so sure the little daughter needed her still. Sleeping or waking her heart yearned to be with her, and often in the night when she awoke, the baby voice would be ringing in her ears, calling her to come. That was a dry aching feverish unassuageable grief, on which ordinary consolation had no power. It might have killed her with its gnawing carking care, but for the gentler sorrow of the other loss, which vented itself naturally in tears, and the tears relieved the over-burdened heart, easing it and strengthening it for the stronger grief.

Then, too, there was George to share her sorrow, and sorrows are less crushing when they are not borne alone. And there were friends who came to see her and strove to console. Utterly futile as was all they could say, their presence and their sympathy were grateful. It is so desolate after awhile to have to bear our wretchedness all alone. An ear in which to pour our complaints, an eye to look pitifully on our pain, soothes and strengthens, if it cannot mitigate the anguish. And Mary had these. Her nephew Ralph Herkimer and his wife were, as the servants said, most attentive : and the sympathy of the wife at least was very genuine, while Ralph's was equally well expressed. And after all, till men become able to read each other's souls—a state of things which even the best of us would not relish—it is the expression which is efficacious or otherwise, not the prompting spirit. Consider it, oh ye of the hard shell, who plume yourselves on your good hearts and sweet natures! How many a cocoanut has been left to rot, because the eaters could not penetrate the husk!

Mary's sisters, too, when they heard of her desolation, had relented; and found they must forgive her having married against their wish. Being human, even if peculiar, they could not but be sorry, only they had said so many things in their heat that each felt awkward about proposing to the other to relax the estrangement so far as to call on the offender. Public opinion, however decided the matter. Mary's distress was perfectly well known to every one, and when the ladies of their acquaintance began to inquire for their sister and to express sympathy, it was even more "awkward" to acknowledge the estrangement than to bring it to an end.

Circumstances were kind to them in their attempt to make friends, and let them down very gently. When they called the first time their sister was far too ill to see any one, which spared them the "awkwardness" of a meeting. They called every day afterwards, and so had their bulletin ready for inquiring friends, and also had their own feelings modulated gradually to a gentler frame. By-and-by they were admitted to the sickroom. Mary was too feeble to talk; she welcomed them with a faint smile, to which the only possible answer on their part was a kiss, a kiss of reconciliation as well as sympathy, all the more reconciling in that no words were possible on either side, for so soon as it was given the nurse was ready to usher them out again without parley.

On the late October day we have mentioned Mary lay with her thin fingers twined about the baby's plaything, and tears stealing from her eyes. As each movement of her chest stirred the little bells, their ringing thrilled her senses like a pain.

It was the far-away cry of a departed joy, reminding her of its loss. And yet she clasped the bauble but the tighter for each new sting it inflicted on her heart; it brought the vanished past a little nearer, and she almost coveted the pain as a relief from the leaden desolation under which she lay. So, when a wound begins to heal, one will touch and trifle with it, reviving the smart as an easement from the weary numbness of the congested tissues. She was absorbed in her sorrowful musings and did not note the entrance of her sisters, till, in their sabled gowns, coming between her and the light, they bent over her. Susan kissed her on the forehead, and Judith's tightened lips delivered a peck upon her mouth. Then she opened her eyes with a wan smile, and faintly bade them

8—2

welcome, endeavouring to raise herself the while.

"Keep still, Mary," said Susan. "Do not attempt to move. You will get strong all the sooner for taking care now."

"I think," said Judith, observing the child's coral in her hands, which she was at the moment slipping away among her coverings, "you should put away those things. They can do no good, and can only revive distressing thoughts."

Mary sighed, and asked if they had walked.

"Give it to me, Mary!" persisted Judith the energetic, "and let me put it away and lock it up."

"Oh, no!" said Mary, clasping it with both hands to her breast, and smiling sorrowfully. "It comforts me."

"Very wrong! Foolishly injudicious in Mr. Selby to allow it," and Miss Judith stood up with a jerk, as though she would take the obnoxious article by force. "Susan——"

"Judith! Better let alone," her sister interrupted, attempting to draw her back to her chair.

Judith flushed hotly. Like other zealous reformers of their neighbours, she was irritably intolerant of advice to herself; because, of course, she must be right—she always was.

So are the others. She turned upon her sister with a frown, and there might have been words; but at that moment the click of the gate-latch sounded. The gate opened, and a clergyman appeared — a young clergyman. Judith admired clergymen, and we all admire youth, at least all who have lost their own.

By the time the Reverend Dionysius Bunce entered the room, Miss Judith's angry flush had cooled down, and her tightened lips had relaxed into a smile of virgin sweetness. She had a taste for clergymen, just as some other ladies have a taste for horses, and some for cats. People talk of " pigeon-fanciers." Miss Judith was a parson - fancier, that is, she fancied the parsons but she could not keep them, as the pigeon-fanciers keep *their* pets; they always flew away to fresher fields. Mr. Bunce was curate of St. Wittikind's, the church where Selby was organist and choir-master. It was a place of worship which Miss Judith's pietistical scruples would not allow her to attend. The people there were given to singing harmoniously words which she held should be said discordantly, and to other practices equally to be regretted. St. Wittikind's, in fact, was " high," and she never mentioned it without drawing a long breath, and shaking her head sadly. Still, if her mind was controversial it was also feminine, and the curate's trim, ecclesiastical uniform attracted her much. The linen was so white, so tight, and so starchy, while that of the married curate of her own St. Silas' was yellow, limp, and even slovenly, like the services in which he assisted. No doubt it was right, from her standpoint, that the service should be bald and unattractive, and she had very decided views about vestments *in* church, but in vesture *out* of church, she had a woman's preference for neatness, and if she could win this young man from his unevangelical vagaries, would it not be like plucking a brand from the burning? She had long known him by sight, as indeed, she knew all the clergy, but hitherto he had been one of the black sheep in her eyes. Now, when she met him in a room, he was so neat and seemed so young and inexperienced, that her heart yearned towards him with a mother's interest—no! not a mother's interest precisely, but an interest of the adaptable kind, which may change into any other sort as occasion dictates.

In Miss Susan's eyes the curate appeared uninteresting enough. She thought him stubby, commonplace, and scarcely a gentleman, save that to a good churchwoman like herself, his orders, like the Queen's commission in the army, made his position unassailable. But then, Miss Susan had no enthusiasm, and was disposed to let the brands burn, each in its own fashion. She would have liked to go now, when she saw the clergyman sit down beside Mary's sofa, and pull out his book, and had risen with that intention, when Judith, clasping her black gloves and smiling with grave sweetness, as one may smile at a christening, asked if it was absolutely needful that they should go away. "For herself," she said, "there was no portion of our beautiful liturgy in which she so much delighted as in those sweet and improving passages which occur in the 'visitation of the sick,' and if Mr. Bunce did not object, she would feel it a privilege to be permitted to remain."

Poor Mr. Bunce could only acquiesce, and go on with his function, resigning the hope of whatever satisfaction he might otherwise have found in its performance, and a good deal disturbed by Miss Judith's sighs of extreme interest in one place, and the fervency of her responses in another. Susan, too, perforce sat down again, wondering internally at the queerness of her sister's taste. For herself, she felt perfectly well, and it only depressed her to listen to the curate's words. She looked out of the window where the sun was shining, and could not but think that it would have been far more cheerful to be walking down the street.

Having finished, Mr. Bunce would have liked to remain a little for a quiet chat with Mrs. Selby; but Miss Judith sat still and seemed bent on taking on herself the entire duty of conversing with him. It might be well intended, he thought, to save her sister fatigue, but it was not very interesting, so he quickly rose to leave. Judith did so at the same time, and when he reached the gate, the reverend man discovered that fate had condemned him to accompany the two ladies along more than a mile of suburban street, where he saw no hope of breaking away.

# CHAPTER VIII.

## RALPH.

It was with a sweet and respectful smile that Judith looked at the curate, and left him to make the first observation. She would have liked to look up to him; that being her natural mental attitude to men of his cloth; but physically the thing was impracticable. She was not notably a tall woman, but he was distinctly a short man; and though too bulky to be called little, his figure justified Susan's mental definition of him as "stumpy." He was her junior too, and his countenance was not impressive. It was blond as regarded hair and eyes, indefinite in feature, pasty in complexion; still, it was neatly kept, and relieved from vacuity by that undoubting self-complacency which comes to those privileged to reprove and exhort unchallenged, for twenty minutes at a stretch.

Mr. Bunce waited, coughed, observed on the fineness of the weather, and was silent.

Miss Susan agreed with him in her mind, but having nothing to say on the subject, said nothing, and it was left for Judith to fan the verbal spark, and nurse it into a conversation. She opened in dulcet tones, and with a respectful effusiveness, like the carved nymphs round an old fountain, catching the wasting driblets in their marble shells. She agreed that the weather was indeed extremely pleasant, and counted up how many other fine days there had been that week and the week before. But there had been a shower the week before that, just when the people were leaving the missionary meeting, where the good Bishop of Rara Tonga spoke so sweetly. Had Mr. Bunce been there? No? Ah! then, he had indeed missed a treat. It had been most instructive. The bishop told about a deacon who remembered having eaten part of his grandmother, and about the octopus coming out of the sea, to eat breadfruit on shore on moonlight nights,—perhaps it was not breadfruit, by the way, it may have been something else ; and perhaps it was not an octopus; but at any rate it was some dreadful creature, and it did something very curious, and it was all most interesting ; " and indeed, Mr. Bunce, you missed a treat."

Mr. Bunce said he found his parochial duty

too heavy and too engrossing to admit of desultory meeting-going.

"But the heathen! Mr. Bunce, if you take no interest in the octopus."

"We have heathens in Montreal, Miss Herkimer, as ignorant of good as any South Sea Islander. They want to be taught, and some even to be fed, for work is scarce this year, and winter coming on."

"Ah, yes!" answered Miss Judith, "it is sad to think of, and," she added—with a twinge of conscience for what she was about to say, for she was of St. Silas, and set no great store by the church activities of St. Wittikind, but then good manners and Christian charity require one to stretch a point verbally sometimes—"You are doing much good in St. Wittikind's, I understand. We in St. Silas are doing what we can too. We distribute fifty thousand gospel leaflets every month, and with —well, they must have the best results. So many benighted Romanists have no other opportunity to get a glimpse of the truth; and you know, Mr. Bunce, the truth *must* prevail."

"No doubt, Miss Herkimer, it will, some-day. In St. Wittikind's parish, however, we find so many in physical want, and so many with no religion at all, that our hands are full, and we do not attempt controversy."

Miss Judith sighed softly, so as not to be observed. These were not the views in vogue at St. Silas, and of course they were wrong; but with her "yearning" towards this curate, who seemed meet for better things, if he could be won, it seemed her duty to be winning. So she suppressed her inclination to say something " sound," merely observing that all souls were alike precious, and then added that she had heard much of the zealous beneficence exercised at St. Wittikind's, and " would he explain about those sisterhoods, of which people talked so much."

This, to use an Americanism, "fetched" the curate—fetched him round, as it were, to his own shopdoor, the pulpit, into which he at once stepped, and held forth fluently and minutely, and at very great length, while Judith listened with interest. Not so Susan, who found the prelection both tedious and unnecessary. She paid what she thought she could afford to the different charities recommended by her church, whose business she considered it to see that its member's money was well applied; and having paid, she took a receipt in full from her conscience, and did not wish to hear any more about giving till that day twelvemonths, when, if convenient, she would renew the contribution. Every one, she said, had her own preference in fancy-work and amusements; hers was Berlin wool —as indeed her drawing-room showed, where every chair and ottoman was bedecked with representations of impossible herbage in the crudest of colour and design. Judith's fad was handing tracts to ragged French and Irish men, an equally harmless exercise, though with less result to show, seeing the recipients hardly waited till her back was turned before lighting their pipes with them.

Susan's eyes strayed from one passer-by to the next, in search of something to interest her more than the clerical monologue proceeding at her side, and by-and-by she espied a gentleman being driven in the direction from which she had come. An idea struck her; she hailed the cab, which stopped before her, and the gentleman within looked out inquiringly.

"Oh! Mr. Jordan," she said, "forgive my stopping you; but this was the day that wretched woman who stole our little niece was to be tried, and I know you have charge of Mr. Selby's interests in the matter. Is the case decided? What have they done with her? Has she confessed?"

"She has been acquitted, ma'am. I am just now on my way to Mrs. Selby's, who will no doubt be impatient to hear the result; though, for myself, I have suspected for some time there was a mistake in arresting her."

"Acquitted? But the nurse-girl swore positively—did she not?—that that was the squaw who was at the house! And the ferry-boatmen corroborated what she said."

"Yes. The man swore that a squaw with a bundle, which he suspected might be a baby, crossed in the steamboat that afternoon, and he was inclined to swear to the identity of the blanket the prisoner wore, on account of its being torn at one corner. The girl Lisette was very positive about both the blanket and the wearer, and I fear her being so will materially prejudice any further attempts we may make, for the priest swore to the squaw's having been in Caughnawaga all day, and he produced the school roll of the Ladies of the Sacred Heart to show that she had not only been there, but had taken the medal of honour that day."

"Ah! ejaculated Judith with emphasis, "what a system is Popery! So insidious! So soul-destroying!—capable of any subterfuge. I wonder you don't take out a warrant and have that convent searched."

Mr. Bunce opened his eyes, startled and shocked that one so much interested in works of beneficence should have so little charity.

Mr. Jordan, who knew the lady better, sniffed impatiently but not loud, as recognizing the ebullition to be constitutional and unworthy of notice. "The worst of it is," he said, " the girl has sworn so positively that it will weaken the value of her testimony when we bring her up by-and-by to identify the real offender, if found. And we have no other witness to produce. In my professional experience I have always found that too much zeal is dangerous—far worse than too little! How do *you* find it, Mr. Bunce in *your* profession? Zeal without knowledge, eh?" and he glanced with a sly smile from Miss Judy's face to the curate's.

The curate looked blankly before him. He was too slightly acquainted with the ladies to feel warranted in poking fun at their eccentricities; and he was too much of a cleric to welcome a layman's jest on subjects pertaining to his cloth. It was well, he thought, that the lady should have a zeal, whether wise or the reverse. The trouble he had found had oftener been to kindle a zeal than to direct it, and he doubted not but with judicious guidance this ardent lady might be brought right—that is, to take views like his own of most things.

The pause resulting from Mr. Jordan's wit and the curate's unresponsiveness was broken by Miss Susan, who was growing restless. Though no longer young, she retained some of the characteristics of her departed youth, and had what, to misquote the high-heeled dignitaries of literature, might be called "the modern spirit." Had she been thirty years younger than the family bible showed her to be she would assuredly have said that all men of the professions—especially successful ones —were prigs, and most of them bores into the bargain; and, as it was, she thought it. Foolish old woman! Her weakness, in days of old had been for the red coats, and though none of them had ever proposed, she was still loyal to her ancient ideal. Her roving eye descried her nephew Ralph on the other side of the way, and just as the pause incident to the curate's silence became notable, she called aloud, "Ralph!" and waved her parasol.

Ralph obeyed the signal, and joined the party on the curbstone, around the cab door.

"Ah, Ralph!" cried Mr. Jordan. "Going to call on your aunt, I daresay, and tell her the trial is over and that it is proved now we have been on a wrong scent these last three

months, and must begin all over again from
the beginning. Here, get in ; we may as well
go together—or, better still, I will yield you
up the cab. You can explain it all, just as
well as I could ; it seems like a fresh disappointment to the poor lady, and the news
will come better from a relative." Then,
looking at his watch, " I have a meeting due
in ten minutes from now ; I shall still be in
time ; so good-bye! and thanks."

" No—you—don't! Mr. Jordan," responded
Ralph. " I will not deny that I intended to
call at Selby's ; but, since *you* are so far on
your way, just complete the trip. Take all
the credit yourself and charge it in your bill.
I can't do that, you know, being only a
broker."

Jordan looked disgusted, re-seated himself
in his cab and drove away. Susan repeated
her expressions of regret at what she still
looked on as a miscarriage of justice ; but
Ralph replied :

" Not at all! No one who was present at
the trial could have looked for any other
conclusion. We must just try again ; but
—now that old Jordan is out of hearing, one
may venture to say it—the whole case has
been mismanaged. Why did they not offer a
reward at the first? Now, I fear, it will be

too late! The little circumstances which
detectives are able to piece together to so
good a purpose are soon forgotten, and so
the clue is lost."

"Poor Mary!" said Susan, "my heart
bleeds for her. It may turn out for the
best, perhaps, and remedy the iniquity of
Gerald's preposterous will, by keeping the
money in his own family, but it is very sad.
She seems crushed. If her boy had been
spared to her—but to lose them both! It is
turning her hair grey. She who used to be
the flower of our family!"

Judith's lips tightened at "flower of the
family." Herself was that interesting blossom
she thought, but that was not what she said.
On the contrary she expressed herself with
evangelical superiority to such trifles.

"*I* regard it as a dispensation, to wean her
from earthly joys. It is in love that, when
we make ourselves idols, they are taken
away. Perhaps, too, it may be a judgment
on her for marrying in defiance of those who
were older and wiser than herself. There are
warnings in all these mysterious happenings,
and food for thought;" and she rolled her
eyes Sibyl-wise over Ralph to the curate.

There was an irreverent gleam in Ralph's
eyes, and he turned to watch a passing dray

till his inclination to laugh went off. The curate was regarding her with a puzzled expression. He was a well-meaning young man, who wished both to be and to do good; but who, not being any wiser than his neighbours, notwithstanding the higher ground on which, in right of his orders, he believed himself to stand, was often in doubt both as to what he ought to feel and to say. He was very sure it would never have occurred to himself to use the language he had listened to, and he began to wonder if he had stumbled on some advancedly serious person, whose acquaintance would be improving, or —or something else. There seemed a fine devotional tone in her opening words, especially enunciated as they were, with a full and rounded unction. They were not very novel, perhaps; he seemed to have heard the like before, and more than once; but then, what that is true is also new?—as was said, or something not unlike it in sound, by a late prime minister. Her next proposition rather startled him, carrying him back to his college days, and reminding him of the stealing of Jove's thunderbolts; but there was a third—like the third course beloved by another prime minister, reconciling contradictions and committing to nothing—" mys-

9—2

terious happenings, food for thought." That
was it! He would think it over; and there
was balm in this, for had she not been
listening to him, as they came along, as to
another Gamaliel, while he described the
charitable schemes of St. Wittikind's? and
would it not be painful to think otherwise
than well of so responsive a lady?

Confused by all these thoughts the curate
did not speak; and Susan, thinking it high
time to break up the meeting, reminded
Judith that their dressmaker lived hard by,
and now would be a good opportunity to
order their winter gowns. Judith said good-
bye regretfully and made the curate promise
to come very soon and tell her more about
St. Wittikind's, and the two gentlemen walked
townwards together.

"You seem to know my aunt well," said
Ralph. "I am agreeably surprised. I fancied
she was too grimly Low Church to speak to
any clergyman not of St. Silas or St. Zebedee.
I hope your acquaintance will broaden her
views, which are rather extreme, and something of a nuisance in the family. However,
Aunt Judy means well. We all allow that.
The trouble is that she will never allow that
*we* mean well, when we go counter to her
advice; and then she treats us to a word in

season, which is apt to be very highly sea-
soned with brimstone and what not."

There was a tone of levity and indifference
to his cloth in this talk which jarred on Mr.
Bunce. It was evident that Ralph looked
on him as just like a secular person, or perhaps as less shrewd, and this was not as he
liked. His associations were mostly with
the docile of the other sex, and the more
reverential of his own, and the company of
this robust worldling was so unpleasantly
bracing that they soon parted, and Ralph was
alone when he reached his office.

"A man waiting to see you, sir."

"What sort of man?"

"An Indian. The same I think who came
for your guns last year, when you went
camping out."

"Tell him I've gone out."

"He saw you come in through the glass
door."

"Say I'm engaged."

"He says he will wait till you are at
leisure."

"Bid him come in, then," and presently
Paul stood before his employer, looking in
his eyes but saying nothing.

"Well, Paul?" said Ralph, without looking
up from the letter he appeared to be writing,

" deer have been seen near the Lake of Two Mountains, eh? Too busy! Shall not be able to leave town this Fall. Hard on a man —is it not? Wish I was an Indian and could do as I pleased."

" Ouff," grunted Paul, with an impatient glance, and that slight twitch of the eyebrows equivalent to a Frenchman's shrug, which says so plainly " Why all these idle words?" Then, producing a paper from his bosom he handed it to Ralph.

" Ze notaire gave dis! Want pay—for Thérèse—Judge court defend."

" Ah!" said Ralph, taking the paper and glancing over it. " Your bill of costs. Defending that squaw—eh? You want me to look it over?—Oh yes! quite right. O.K!* all correct! Pay it at once, Paul, and finish the business."

" Ze dollars?" answered Paul. " You give! I pay."

" It's all right, Paul! The account, I mean. But you must pay your own bills, you know—defend your own family. She's your squaw, not mine."

Paul shot a fiery glance from under his

---

* All right. First used by an auditor of accounts in Kentucky, who it was believed meant the letters to stand for Oll Kreck (all correct).

gathered brows. "Zis my squaw sister!
Done for you!—O.K? Squaw get dollars for
fetch back papoose. Easy fetch back."

"What do you mean, Paul? What will
be so easy for you to fetch back?" said
Ralph wheeling round in his chair.

"Fetch papoose. Got no dollars for pay
notaire."

"Man alive! Did I not pay you as I
promised?"

"Fifty dollars! O.K! Squaw take papoose
for pay. Notaire want sixty-five. Squaw
bring back papoose. Get two hundred
dollars. Pay notaire. O.K.!"

"Come now, Paul!" cried Ralph, not over
well pleased, yet with a business man's
pleasure in a bit of smartness, even when it
told against himself. "You've euchred me,
I allow it. But don't draw the string too
tight in case it breaks. What do you
want?"

"Two hundred dollars," said Paul.

"But the bill of costs is only sixty-five."

"How long live squaw and papoose on
hundred dollars?" •

"You leave thirty-five out of the reckon-
ing. However, we will suppose that goes to
you for your smartness. Well! I'm busy,
Paul, I'll give you your two hundred dollars

at once to get you away. Not, mind you,
that I couldn't fight you off, if I cared
to; but I have other things to think of."

"And for Fidèle and the papoose?"

"That must suffice them for the present.
When it is all spent—we will see—" and so
Ralph got rid of his importunate visitor for
the present, though not without misgiving.

# CHAPTER IX.

SAINT EUPHRASE is a village of the usual Lower
Canada type, with its big high-shouldered stone
church, made stately in front by square towers
capped with tin belfries, on which the light
twinkles as the bell tinkles to call the people
to mass. The village, like a brood of chickens,
nestles around, a cluster of little low-browed
wooden houses, with pillared porches and
verandahs, the poorer ones roofed with
weather-stained shingles, the prosperous with
red plates or tin ; pierced here and there with
little casements, shining yellow in the afternoon sun, like inquisitive eyes prying into
their neighbours' enclosures. A few tall pop-
lars—sign of a French-speaking settlement—
rise here and there above the roofs, and around
are fields divided by picturesquely ill-kept
fences, in whose corners the wild plum or the
slippery elm entwined with brambles form
belts of growth which might be hedges, grate-

ful to the eye after the trim bald farming of
the West.   A broad river runs by at about a
stone-cast's distance, but the place used to be
too small to have traffic by water; and save
to the boatman who got his living by ferrying
people across the river, was but a desert barrier
to the villagers, cutting them off from the
West, whither Transatlantic prosperity ever
tends—lonely waters down which a few rafts
of timber passed in the Spring, and peopled
only by the duck and teal frequenting the
reedy shores of an island down stream, a bank
raised by opposing currents and gathered out of
the flood by a thicket of ash and willow.   The
fields sloping upwards on the other three sides,
end in bush, which would cover the general
level of the country but for the farms, with
their houses set by the roadsides and their
narrow strips of land running for a mile or
more back into the distance.   Of late a good
many country houses have been built by Mon-
trealers desiring something less suburban than
their own island affords.   There is a railway,
and a few modern shops; and gaily-dressed
townspeople may be seen driving fast horses
or playing lawn tennis in the cool of the afternoon; but these are recent innovations on the
old time when M. le Curé in his long skirts
walked down the street alone among the bow-

ing *habitants*, smiling as he went and bestowing his blessing.

"General" Stanley was the earliest outsider to build himself a home in the sequestered neighbourhood, and not many as yet had followed his example, at the time we speak of. If it had been dull in his lifetime, his daughters found it doubly so after his death, and but for the horrors of moving they would have migrated back to the city. As we grow older it becomes ever more painful to root up formed habits, while new ones are less and less able to to take their place ; and Miss Stanley, at least, acknowledged that she had reached the age when change grows irksome. Therefore, while they amused themselves by talking of removal, and each Spring promised themselves the comforts of town life for the succeeding Winter, the years slid by and they found themselves still where they were. The years too made havoc among their circle of friends, and made the city seem a less desirable residence, just as the week works changes in our gardens, scarce noticeable from day to day, but so complete before the month is out. People die and marry and move away, and the ladies' shopping expeditions to Montreal grew briefer and less frequent as time went on, till from lasting over weeks and ending in tender partings from regretful friends, they dwindled into excursions accomplished between a morning and an afternoon. Soon, too, there came into the neighbourhood a sprinkling of English-speaking settlers, which, productive in the end of life and spirit, was like yeast turbid and disturbing at first, when dropped into that sweet but stagnant reservoir of old-world manners ; and soon there was on the outskirts of the village a Protestant mission, a meek little clap-boarded structure, without spire or bell, but sufficient for the needs of its few worshippers, and enough to rouse the watchfulnesss of the curé and the jealous wrath of his flock. However, the parson proved to be a peace-loving man, and the zeal which at first threatened to become flagrant, simmered down for want of provocation, into armed neutrality, if not into more neighbourly feelings. These changes brought the ladies at least the feeling of a less complete isolation than they had experienced at first, and eventually, as the grade of new-comers improved, a little society ; while the earlier polemical excitement passed them by, they being persons content to say their own prayers in their own fashion, and to leave their neighbours to do likewise.

"Oh, Tookey!" said Miss Matilda, when

the sisters met at breakfast on the morning after the arrival of the baby, " the little darling is simply delightful! When I took her upstairs Smithers most obligingly offered to keep her through the night; but it looked so pretty lying fast asleep in my bed with nothing on but a large pocket handkerchief, that I really had not the heart to disturb it. We bathed it, you know, and you cannot think what a dear, soft, plump little morsel it looked in its bath; and it crowed—positively crowed and smiled to me myself, for I do not think it minded Smithers much, though it was she who did the bathing. I daresay her hands felt rough, you know, on its tender little skin. We laid it in my bed and covered it with a pocket-handkerchief—dear little morsel—while I went to look for something small enough to dress it in. I thought of the clothes for my immense wax doll I was so proud of once, and kept so long after I grew up; but alas! I gave that to my godchild, and apparently every rag of its wardrobe; I thought I might find a little shirt or a wrapper—I am certain they would have been quite large enough for this one—but Tilly Martindale seems to have got them every one. Is it not a pity? But, as I was saying, we laid baby in the bed while I was looking for the things, and she just dropped asleep the moment Smithers laid her down. So I just sent Smithers off to bed, and lay down beside the dear little duck, and it has nestled in my arms all night, as soft as a ball of silk ; and oh, Tookey ! I don't think I ever slept as pleasantly before ; and in the morning it woke me by stroking my cheeks with its soft little hands. Did you notice its hands ? I never saw anything so lovely, with a crease round the wrist, a dimple at each knuckle, and pink little finger-tips like rosebuds."

" But what are we to do with the infant ? " asked the practical Penelope.

" Do ? The first thing to do is to give it some bread and milk ! But I daresay Smither's has done that already. I should have liked to do it myself but was afraid to try. I remember so well how I hurt my kitten's mouth, trying to feed it with a teaspoon, and I would'nt make this little beauty cry for all the world. But I know what I will do. I have some cambric for pocket-handkerchiefs upstairs, I shall make it a chemise ! Smithers will know how big to make it, or rather how little—the dear wee love ! "

" Matilda, dearest, let us be sensible. The child must have a *parent*, and if *we* can become attached to it so warmly in a few hours what must the feelings of that parent be to be deprived of her ?   Ought we not to endeavour to return the child ? "

" If the parents valued it so highly why did they leave it here, without asking leave or saying a word ?   No ! They forsook it ! I shall always say so.   Besides, how can we give it back, even if we would try?   How find the discreditable parents?   And if we could, what a life we might be giving up the little lamb to ! "

" It does not seem right, our keeping it."

" And whom, pray, would you give it up to ? Would you give it to the village priest ?— to be carried to some convent and brought up for a nun ?—fasting, and scrubbing all her life long for the sisterhood ?   Just look at the tiny hands, like little flowers, and the plump little person.   Work and fasting, indeed !   Not if *I* can help it."

" But there is the parson.   Naturally we would give it in charge to our own church."

" And how much better would that be ? What could an old bachelor do, but make his housekeeper wrap it in a shawl, and carry it to the Protestant Orphan Home ?   A very good place you know—I have been through it– quite proper for children such as it is meant for — rough little squalling things, quite tough and hardy.   They are cared for, and taught and brought up to service. A most useful institution and I shall double my subscription, but it would be no home for *our* little fairy. Why, it is a blossom! It would wither away in that rough place within a week. And better so, than the desecration of rearing it there! No, no! I shall keep it for my own, if it is not claimed. Of course if we knew its parents, and they were proper people, it would be wrong not to let them know ; but even then I would par them money to let me adopt it. And if they wanted to keep the child, why did they bring it here ? It seems nonsense to think about the parents at all."

" I do not like the idea of keeping a stray baby whom nobody knows anything about, Tilly ! We should ask advice, at any rate. I think I had better go over to Montreal and ask Mr. Jordan what we should do."

" And have yourself laughed at for a fussy old maid, saddled with a baby ! You will make us a laughing stock to all our friends. Just think how ridiculous it sounds ! Besides, what can he advise ? I know quite well what he will say, and can save you your consultation fee. He will ask you to " be seated " in his clients' chair—*I* know, for I visited him several times about my steamboat shares, and it was always the same performance—then he lies back in his own chair and takes his foot upon his knee. After that he takes off his spectacles, wipes them with his handkerchief and puts them on again, rests his elbows on the chair arms, clears his voice and begins, ticking off the items of advice with the fingers of one hand upon those of the other. He makes it very clear, and it sounds most wise; but when you go away and think it over, you will find he has told you just what you might have told yourself, if you had only thought calmly and sensibly about it. There is no witchcraft in Mr. Jordan's advice. Perhaps that is why people say he is a sound lawyer. Remember, too, he is apt to divulge the secrets of her dear friends to his wife. She spoke to *me* about my steamboat shares, I remember; and congratulated me upon selling at the right time. You know how dearly she loves a good story, and if your dilemma should strike her in an absurd light, she will soon have it known all over the town. Our dear Amelia has a very long tongue."

"I only want to do what is right," said Penelope, a little dismayed at the suggestion, " right to ourselves, and right to this baby. I feel for the little waif, Tilly, though I do not become rapturous like you."

"As to the baby, then, just think. It seems unlikely that it would have been laid

on our verandah if its friends had wanted to
keep it at home.   Even if we could return it to
them we could not make them keep it, or use
it kindly ;  and there seem to be only three
other ways of disposing of it—the Protestant
Orphans' Home, the Grey Nunnery, or to
adopt it ourselves.   Now, suppose we were
to do the last—I do not propose it, mind ;
but, after there seems no more likelihood of its
being claimed, if we should—would it be
nice to have our *protegée* spoken of as a foundling, and nobody's child ?   Would it not tell
against her when she grew up, and we took
her into society with us, as of course we should
if we reared her ourselves ? "

" But, my dear, the child has not been
twelve hours in the house yet, and to hear
you, one would say you are already dreaming
of bringing it up !  I have known you all your
life, Tilly, and I never heard you discuss at
such length before ; but what you say seems
reasonable enough.   It would *not* be nice to
have Amelia making fun of our perplexities,
and yet there is no one else we can go to, whose
advice we could trust in like Mr. Jordan's.
For yourself, now, what do you think we
should do ? "

" I think we should do nothing !  Nobody
can blame us for doing that.   It is no affair

of ours, and if only we are kind to the little one till a claimant appears, or till we see more plainly what we should do, we can get nothing but praise and thanks for our charity."

To do nothing is always an inviting course, in times of perplexity, especially when it is the interest of another rather than our own which is most deeply involved ; we cannot then be blamed for doing the wrong thing, even if we have failed to do the right one. Time, too, has a way of winding up affairs left open, which is often more satisfactory than the half-wise efforts of meddlesome mortals. Miss Stanley accepted the invitation to inaction and let things take their course.

That day was a royal one for Miss Matilda. Instead of loitering between her flowers and her sofa, fanning herself and dropping asleep, a new interest had come into her life ; and such a pretty one ! It crept and rolled and tumbled about on the matting at her feet ; while she sat at her worktable in the bay window with scissors and cambric, sewing strange garments, and pricking her fingers a good deal, for the needle was an unfamiliar implement in her hands ; but she went bravely on with unflagging industry, stopping only to get fresh bread and milk, when she imagined the little one must be hungry, or to find a pillow when it wanted to sleep.

10—2

The newspapers came in the afternoon as usual, but she had no leisure to waste on them; the plaything at her feet was far too engrossing. Even Penelope only glanced over the column of " Born," "Died "and "Married " —there is no " Divorced " in a Canadian paper, as in American ones—in search of any known name, and then sat down to wonder at Matilda's new-born energy and admire the baby.

These ladies were not very thorough-going newspaper readers, although they lived in the country and saw few visitors. The two city newspapers they received each day were always torn open, the marriages and deaths glanced at, and sometimes the fashions, if it was their time for getting new bonnets; but politics bewildered them, and the local gossip had ceased to be interesting, it was so long since they had lived in town. Their bookseller sent them magazines and boxes of books, their home was comfortable, and life moved on smoothly, like a door on well-oiled hinges. They forgot to crave for outside interests and excitements, and the energies which in town life might have found scope in arranging or disarranging their neighbours' concerns, took gentler exercise over roses, geraniums, chickens, bees, or a rheumatic habitant, especially if he spoke prettily and was respectful.

It was only as might be expected, then, that nothing in the newspapers relating to their little waif ever met their eyes. The parson—their only visiting neighbour at that time—was away for his summer vacation; the friends who sometimes came to them from Montreal were at the seaside, so there was no one to talk with, and they heard nothing ; which indeed was as they liked it best. All through the remainder of that Summer and Golden Fall, these two women, not very young, revelled in a new-found joy—the sudden awakening within them of the holy instinct of mother-hood—the double living, living in another life besides their own, the joyous wondering pro-gressive life of childhood—re-entering anew a world still dew-bright in the morning fresh-ness which it loses as life wears on; and their hearts grew purer and their thoughts simpler, in this unlooked for return to the Eden of long ago.

Before two months had passed they had come to recognize their little visitor as a member of the household and one of the family—"of our own family, sister," Matilda said one day. " Let us make her a Stanley and call her our niece—Muriel Stanley. What do you say ? "

" But how can we, with neither brother nor

sister, call her that?" said Penelope the
business-minded and literal. "Think of the
stories we should have to make up; and if
anybody asked questions we should have
to make some more, and there would be dis-
crepancies, and the most dreadful things
might be said."

"And pray," cried Matilda the impetuous,
"who will presume to ask questions when we
look them in the eye and calmly state the—
the fact that she is our brother's child, and he
is dead? Some people are not very polite, but I
never met any one who would dare to dis-
believe a lady to her face ; and if we give no
particulars and change the subject at once,
there will be no opportunity to ask questions,
If we call it a niece there will be no more to
say, and as soon as it is generally known it
will interest nobody. They are all too full
of their own affairs."

"But, Tilly, we never had a brother."

"But, Tookey dear, who knows that? Papa
married in this country, and you were born
here, but you know he was sent to Bermuda
soon after, and we remained there till you and I
were grown. Nobody in Montreal knows even
that mamma was Canadian. Nobody asks anything about the connections of the military or
commissariat. There they are. The Service is

a voucher for their respectability. It is taken for granted that they are English with no relations in this country, so nobody troubles to inquire."

"But our mother's relations, Tilly, in Upper Canada; what are we to say to *them?*"

"We have been thirteen years in Canada without meeting them. Mamma had only a sister—Aunt Bunce—who died before we left Bermuda; if her family live in Upper Canada still, they cannot know much about us. It is so long since poor mamma died—before Aunt Bunce, even—so very long that I do not care to count the years; it makes me feel so old."

"Don't talk of being old, child! You have not aged one bit. Think of me! But why need we bother with telling fibs about the child? Fibs always end in bother; I have been taught that all my life."

"Do you want us to be laughed at? Are you willing to confess yourself an old maid —a Protestant grey nun—adopting babies left on your doorstep? I am not, if you are; though I suppose I *am* older to-day than I was five years ago," and she shook out her ringlets with a defiant toss. "Just let it become generally known that we keep an upper-class foundling asylum, and we shall soon get plenty of pupils! They will bring them from Vermont, I daresay, or up from Quebec."

"Tush! Tilly."

"It is true. Only how should we dispose of them after they were brought up? Other institutions train them for service; now I do not think we could do that, so what would become of them? And what will become of our own little pet if we let her be looked on as a stray, and different from other children? Think of the slights she will be exposed to; and the unkind remarks, especially as she is sure to be pretty. It would be cruelty to bring her up with ourselves, and yet deprive her of the chance of marrying. Think of her struggles as a lonely woman to support herself after we are gone. Our gentle nurture would prove a curse to her and not a blessing."

"But we could not let a gentleman marry a nameless girl under a false impression."

"Certainly not. We would explain all to any gentleman who had a right to know; and if he *was* a gentleman, I do not think it would prevent the marriage; but that is quite different from proclaiming a poor girl's misfortune."

"Think the matter over, Penelope, and I am sure you will come to see it as I do.

Meanwhile there is no hurry. We need not converse to visitors about our *protégée*, she is too little yet to be shown to company, and as the weather is growing cold, I propose we arrange that room at the top of the house as a nursery, and establish her there with Smithers. She will be out of the way both of draughts and idle curiosity."

# CHAPTER X.

TEN years later. What a startlingly abrupt
transition for the onlooker from the " then"
to the " now!" And yet how intimately the
two are connected, and how utterly the one
is dependent on the other! Two cities on the
same broad river, the upper spreading along
the stream, set in a fruitful plain, the key to
fertile regions farther up, gathering the produce and shipping it down the current; the
other perched upon cliffs and overhanging
shores, and twice each day lapped by the
turning tide from the distant sea whither
everything is tending. Yet to the voyager
the transition is gradual enough, and smooth,
and natural. But for the retreating objects
along the shore he would not recognize that
he was moving, save when descending a rapid,
or running on a sandbank—the events, marriages, deaths, failures, and successes of his
onward way. It is the same river still, in

part the very drops of water which tumbled over Niagara long ago, passed through Ontario, and down the rapids to Montreal, and onward through the broads and the deeps till it meets tide-water at Quebec, and still with all the gathered tributes it hurries on, a river still for scores and scores of miles between ever widening banks, on to the misty everlasting sea, where the voyager disappears for ever from the view.

Not that my friends have moved their dwelling-place down stream to Quebec, but there is a sadness in the thought of the slowly passing years which makes one moralize and grow metaphoric before he is aware. No, the people of this history are still geographically where they were, standing on their own ground, while the big tumultuous river rushes by—but the figure which their permanence suggests is even a sadder one, that of the fabled maidens drawing water in their sieves, water which will not be drawn or held, but keeps oozing through and slipping away, just as the stream runs by and will not wait ; for life is but a sorry comedy with its stayless passing. Yet which of us would stop it if we could, even at its best ? It always seems as if a sweeter drop were somewhere up the stream, and even if the present could be held, we would let it pass to taste the fancied sweeter yet to come.

In ten years the American war had ended and specie payments were resumed. In ten years Ralph Herkimer had made a fortune and a "position"—the terms are interchangeable in the moneyed world, and elsewhere too. No one was better liked or more respected as a good fellow, a clear-headed business man, and a high-souled altogether superior person. Even General Considine—who had been taken prisoner during the war, exchanged, "paroled," withdrawn from the game like the slaughtered pawn from a chess board—had quite forgotten having grandly dropped his acquaintance in Natchez and the reasons for so doing; and, on taking up his abode in Montreal, was very pleased to renew intimacy with his young friend of *ante bellum* times. Ralph was happy to respond. If there ever had been an imputation on his courage, it seemed well to support the only one who could remember, in forgetting it; though really, as he told himself, there was nothing to be ashamed of. He had merely shown disapproval of a bloodthirsty and barbarous custom in a state of society already passed away; and no one who was anybody would have the bad taste to be amused at anecdotes told at the expense of a man so well off as himself, and who entertained so liberally. Still, since it is wiser to humour fools than to fight them, he would be civil to this broken-down fireater, heap coals of fire on his head like a good Christian, and make him thoroughly ashamed of his rudeness in former years.

Considine, too, was no very cumbrous *protégé.* He was better supplied with money than many of his compatriots at that time, having inherited some property in New York, which the same events which had ruined his estate in the South had rendered four times as valuable as before, in the paper money of the period. His deportment exhibited a fair share of the manly pathos becoming a fallen hero, and made him an interesting guest to the dwellers in a city at peace. It is true he wore red studs in his shirt front, as his way of mounting his country's colours—red and white—and would defiantly puff out his chest so decorated whenever a Yankee uniform came in sight. But something must be permitted to the bruised susceptibilities of the warrior .overcome, and at least he did not travesty the conspiracies of exiled Poles and old time Jacobites by joining in absurd schemes to capture towns on the lakes, or infect the capital with yellow fever ; in which

crack-brained escapades the excitement for the
plotters lay not so much in their design, as in
communicating it to one another with infinite
stage mystery of whisperings, signs, passwords,
and secret information. In those days a party
of refugees on one of the St. Lawrence steam-
boats would make the voyage as interesting to
their fellow-passengers as a pantomime, with
their dark glances, stealings aside, mysterious
beckonings to each other, and hasty whispers,
followed by backward glances in search of
spies. There may have been real plots, but
they were carried on by practical persons
who showed no sign, and it was rumour of
these which impressed the rest, and filled
them with emulation. They imagined they
were being watched and reported on at Wash-
ington, though what interest their vagaries
could have for Mr. Lincoln's government it is
hard to imagine. Much, however, should be
excused to people deprived by war of their fortunes and their homes, often with but slender
means of support, and no occupation, driven
to spend eight hours of their day in euchre
playing, and the other eight in unending dis-
cussions of the war news. To such, con-
spiracy must have seemed the most delightful
of pastimes, even if barren of practical results.

When Considine approached Ralph with

a most respectable sheaf of "greenbacks", under his arm, and appealed to him as an old friend for advice as to their conversion into specie, and their subsequent employment, Ralph was genial, and by-and-by showed him the way to the gold-room, where good Canadians, following the lead of New York, sold each other stacks of foreign currency which the sellers could not deliver and the buyers had no wish to receive. The telegraph clerk hung up the quotations from New York at certain hours, the "operators" took note and paid their losses—no! "held settlements" is the proper expression, for this was *busi-ness.* Respectable gentlemen, church members, and heads of families, brushed their hats each morning and walked down to their offices, gloved and caned, the very pink of respectability, and from thence went on "'Change," where the money would change hands with astounding celerity—all in the way of "business."

"*Faites votre jeu, Messieurs! Le jeu est fait*"? Not at all! This was in Montreal not at Monte Carlo. Strictly "business," and thoroughly respectable. True, many men lost, but some won. And what would you have? How could it be otherwise? There are but a certain number of gold pieces in the world;

and, if, after an " operation," my bag contains more, it is certain that my neighbour's must hold less. Currency, bullion, stocks, shares, grain, cotton, what are any of them but the tokens to win and lose money upon? But the thing is done " upon 'Change," and 'Change, like church, is a good word, and everything belonging to it is respectable. If it were round a green-cloth table now, how different it would be! though the outcome might be the same. Respectability cannot tolerate the green cloth. And yet, to an all-seeing eye, there may be less amiss when a man's money falls upon the *black* and the *red*. At least the play at Monte Carlo is " on the square;" there are no misquotations or false telegrams, bogus prospectuses, lying reports, collusive understandings, and traps for the unwary, such as have been heard of at times in the places of better repute.

Ralph Herkimer made a great deal of money; Considine made some; and by-and-by, as American finance returned to a normal position, other fields of enterprise were needed as the possibilities of gambling in gold and greenbacks grew less; and then Considine's American connections became a valuable introduction for Ralph to several " good things." There were estates whose owners, stripped of all their other property, and still encumbered by their debts, could not wring a subsistence from the devastated acres, and were willing to part with them for a trifle; but no one would buy—no one at hand, that is, who had opportunity to know about the war-ravaged fields and the intractable labourers. But at a distance, in a land of peace, where a good title and a veracious statement of the acreage and the yielding capacity were the data—where, in fact, a pencil and a piece of paper were the means for judging the promise of the venture—how different it all was. Here was a country where snows and frosts were scarcely known, or, so it was said, where the cattle could range without shelter all through the year, where the gardens were planted with figs and pomegranates, and pigs fattened in the orchards on peaches too plentiful to repay the gathering. There were minerals too, every variety of riches, gold, coal, copper, hidden in the ground, and only awaiting the capital and skill to dig them up; and forests of pine, now vastly enhanced in value by the Chicago fire, waiting to be cut down and converted into lumber if only foreign enterprise would undertake the task. What could be better calculated to stir the imagination of people accustomed to contend for three long months of the

year with the fiercest severities of winter, and
to wring fixed and moderate profits by patient
industry from a soil which still was five or
ten times the price of these fields of endless
summer? The fevers, malaria, bad water, and
general backwardness did not show on the
map, and a dense silence kept them from the
knowledge of investors.

Ralph and his friend being well-to-do, their
statements and recommendations were im-
plicitly accepted; and, indeed, the statements
in themselves were not untruthful; it was in
the counter-balancing facts, which were left
unstated, that those who afterwards considered
themselves their dupes, found the limitation
and disillusion of their hopes, which teach
men in the end that Fortune is as likely
to find them out while labouring at home,
as to be found by them without exertion and
experience, in distant places. But that was
the buyers' concern—knowledge which came
to them later and by degrees. Ralph and
his friend had completed their share of the
transaction and pocketed their commission
when the sale was made; what followed had
for them no interest.

They made many such sales, pocketing large
commissions—the larger, indeed, the worse
the property they disposed of—vast tracts in

some cases, containing untold wealth in minerals and forests, where the buyers sunk fortunes in endeavouring to bring the riches within reach; and at length, having exhausted their resources, had to subside into the ranks of the ruined people around them, and wait patiently for a generation, till the march of time should bring within reach of their children the sums they had placed out of reach for themselves. There were smaller farms, too, where sturdy yeomen with their blooming children went to make rich more quickly; but somehow few appeared to thrive in those distant migrations. Their livestock was apt to die; too little rain, or too much, would destroy their crops, and their own health would fail; and in a year or two they would find their way back to Canada, with an enlarged experience but a shrunken purse; while of the children, some would be left behind in the foreign churchyard, and the rest, yellow and gaunt, bore small resemblance to the bright-eyed youngsters they had been before.

In a few years the trade in southern homesteads died out, Canadian enterprise laid down her telescope and interested herself with things nearer home. Science, ransacking her own soil, had come on hid treasure of

11—2

many kinds, gold, copper, iron, phosphates, and plumbago, and showed where, instead of sending her savings abroad, she might sink them at home—her own savings and those of many a sanguine stranger.　On every side Ralph saw opportunities of money-making, and he was ready to use them; but now his operations, he found, must be on another footing than before.　Hitherto he had been a financier; now, his neighbours recognized him as a capitalist.　The change of standing was gratifying, but it had its dangers and its drawbacks.

Finance has been described as the art of transferring money from one pocket to another—in a Stock Exchange sense, be it understood, not an Old Bailey one—and the financiers are the artists who perform the feat.　Money is a volatile and also an adhesive substance—matter in a state of unstable equilibrium, which must not be disturbed or changes will ensue—wherefore, in the process of transferring, some of it is certain to be spilled, and that the artist may pick up if he can; it is his perquisite.　A good deal too is apt to stick to the artist's fingers—perquisites again—and hence the profit of handling other people's money.　If it were one's own already, whence would come the

profit? A man can scarcely gain by paying
perquisites to himself; though, to be sure, he
may obviate the necessity of paying them to
any one else. But there cannot be a doubt that
the financier escapes much embarrassment
when he is not a capitalist. See, for example,
with what calm unflinching pluck a "general
manager" can carry on war with a rival railway! The next half-yearly dividend may be
sacrificed in the contest, but he does not falter,
he goes bravely on. *He* is not a shareholder;
it makes no matter to *him.* To seek a parallel
in the political world capitalists and financiers
stand to one another as kings to their
ministers. When things go well the minister
does the work, the king has the profit and
glory; but when they miscarry, though the
minister did the mischief, it is the king who
loses his crown; the minister merely with-
draws into privacy, and lives comfortably in
retirement on the emoluments of former office.
Yet who, if he could, would not be a king, to
be trembled before and worshipped? and after
all, the successful revolutions are not numerous.

Ralph recognized the new danger in his
path, and regretted a little, at times, when he
found he must let a profitable opportunity go
by, merely because it was one which only an
impecunious promoter durst undertake; but

he had his compensations. Like the man who becomes a king, he got well grovelled to, and he liked it. He could *influence*, too, if the after responsibilities of " promoting " were too onerous to be undertaken. The use by other men of his name, unauthorizedly, as a heavy holder of their stocks, was worth money ; and, as long as he " unloaded " in time, perfectly safe. He did not now flutter about 'Change, scattering reports and picking up news ; he sat in his office, and was waited on by those who sought his countenance in their schemes and wished to learn its price.

Only one disappointment as yet had befallen him. He wished to become president of a leading bank, and he knew so many of the directors that he made sure of gaining his point. Unfortunately the directors knew him as well, and deemed it advisable to choose some one else ; but then of course it was the general body of shareholders who must bear the blame. The ballot leaves so many things in doubt, and covers up so much about which there can be no doubt at all. His friends, the directors, called on him immediately the election was over—the traitors being probably the first to hurry in—and expressed the most cordial regret and condolence ; and Ralph was too wise not to accept the profuse explana-

tions with gracious condescension. Their
hastening to explain was a tribute, at any rate,
to his weight, and showed that they feared
him; and as one after another he smiled them
out, he promised himself to let them feel yet
that their fears had not been groundless. He
was not, therefore, in his most debonair mood,
when, on being informed by a new clerk that
a rough-looking man had been waiting some
time, he permitted him to be introduced.

"Paul?"

"—— day, sir."

"It seems only the other day since you
were here last."

"Six months."

"How many six months do you make in
a year?"

"Two."

"Hm—I am not so sure of that. Seems
to me you have managed to pack three into
this last year. However—Here, Stinson!" he
called to the clerk appointed to wait without
and attend his private behests, while he
scribbled a cheque. "Ask the cashier to cash
that. Quick!" he added as he raised his
eyes and saw the stolid figure of his visitor
standing before him, a statue in copper-
coloured flesh, motionless and unregarding,
unimpressed by his grandeur or the trembling

assiduousness of his clerk ; an embodiment of
still impassible waiting, like the image carved
on the granite door-post of an Egyptian
temple.  Paul did not even glance about
him, he simply stood, and with unwinking
eye gazed into space, inscrutible and indifferent to all around.

Ralph threw himself back in his chair,
fidgetted impatiently, and coughed and
snorted.  So impressive is that which cannot
be gauged or looked into, even if it contain
nothing.  This was the instrument, too, and
the reminder of a crime, who stood before
him ; a crime of so long ago, and which yet,
so long as the Indian lives may come to light
—may even be remedied, and leave him
unprofited by the deed, as well as disgraced
by its discovery.  With wonder he asked himself how he could have ventured to do
what he had done, the chances of failure
being so many, the consequences of detection
so ruinous, that to think of them even now
sent a cold thrill through him.  Since it was
done, however—and he felt no remorse at the
deed—he was content enough to enjoy the
fruits, although his successes since had made
him in a measure independent of them ; still
his uncle's millions when they came—came to
his boy that is, but he ere then would be his

partner—would, added to his own, gain him
a position above rivalry; and even now in
expectancy they enhanced his importance.

Stinson returned with the proceeds of the
cheque, and Ralph counted over two hundred
dollars to hand to Paul. His fingers lingered
lovingly over the bits of paper, touching each
dollar with a dainty caress as though he loved
it and was sad to part.

It is strange how a rich man hates to part
with money, while the poor are free and even
lavish so far as their little " pile " will go ; but
perhaps we only invert the statement of what
is a truism, that they who dislike to part with
their money keep it and grow rich, while they
who spend it lavishly grow poor. At any rate,
Ralph lingered while he counted the two hundred dollars, and the thought occurred to him
" how many times more would this have to be
done ? " Eight years still before Gerald's
money became payable ! Sixteen more half-
yearly payments of two hundred dollars each !
Thirty-two hundred dollars in all, besides interest ! It seemed monstrous. Could nothing
be done ? Could he not be made to take a
round sum down, and be bound to keep silence
for ever ? No ! That had been tried already,
and so soon as the money was spent he came
back for more, saying he must live, and if

Ralph would not pay, assuredly the bereaved parents would. And so it had come about that Paul was grown an annuitant, and came to claim his little income every six months.

"Here you are, Paul," growled Ralph, handing over the money with a sigh ; and Paul with a gleam in his eye laid hands upon the roll of bills which vanished from view forthwith.

"Say, Paul," speaking in a more insinuating voice, "would it not suit you better to get a good big lump of money once for all, than to be coming here so often drawing it by dribs and drabs ? If I were to give you a thousand dollars now, all at once, see how many things you could do with it! You could open a tavern up the Ottawa and make your fortune right away, and you would save all the money you spend for drink besides."

"Ah!" said Paul, his face lighting up at the inviting picture, and bending forward with extended palm to receive the largess at once.

"I con-sent !"

"Consent to what ?"

"Take ze money."

"Of course you will, my fine fellow ; I know that. And after you have got rid of it all you will come back to me for more."

"Promise to come no more."

"Of course you do! But you will come all

the same. The promise don't count after the money is spent. I have not forgot last time."

Paul smiled like a man who receives a compliment. Veracity was not his point of honour. Rather, it was smartness ; and to have " done " this rich and masterful white man seemed an achievement to be proud of. He stroked his beardless cheeks with a simper of gratified vanity, and fairly laughed at last, so tickled was he by the recollection of his cleverness.

" No ! my fine fellow, you don't come it over me again like that !—no use supposing it. But I'll tell you what I *will* do, for I like you, you see, Paul ; though I know you're a rascal. I have been thinking that if that child were to die it would be bad for you. You could not try it on with me any more by threatening to carry the kid home to its people, and so your pension would come to an end, and you'd have to go to work. How would you like that, Paul, you idle dog, after all these years ? So I have been thinking that if that were to happen —the kid's death, you know—and you could bring me some proof, I would give you a lump sum and have done with you."

" If the papoose die ? "

" Yes."

" You give thousand dollars ? — dollars down ? "

" Down on the nail, if you bring proof."

" How make sure ? "

" You will tell me how it all happened, and I shall know how to verify the fact."

" No, no! Make *me* sure. Thousand dollars."

" Ha! I see. You want some assurance that I will pay what I say? Don't see what more assurance I can give than to say so, or what more you should want. Have I not kept my word with you before ? "

" Ouff "—and Paul plunged into thought where he stood, while Ralph, impatient to be rid of him, collected his papers and locked them in his desk, rose, and took his hat and gloves, as if about to go home.

This brought Paul's reflections to a point. He turned to Ralph with a grin and a grunt, and held out his hand.

" Thousand dollars! " he said with another grunt ; and when Ralph, supposing it a fashion of leave-taking, laid some of his fingers rather gingerly on the extended palm, he caught and shook them eagerly, saying :

" Pay down! Pay down! Papoose dead."

Ralph drew back.

" Dead! When? Where? Tell me all about it."

" Dead at Caughnawaga."

" How long ago ? "

" Ten year—Day 'twas took. Come, see, if you will. *Au-dessous du plancher* at my *cabane*—Thousand dollars ! " and he held out his hand again.

"Ten years ago ! And you have been drawing money from me for that child's support all this time ? And never told ! "

Paul looked gratified, and drew himself up like modest genius when at length its merit is brought to light. Then he chuckled and moved his fingers as if to poke Ralph in the ribs. The idea of Ralph's having been so completely fooled was too delicious.

"But how could it have happened? You cannot mean that you—murdered the child ? "

" Ouff," grunted Paul, from whose face the grin was fading. His sly escapade appeared not to be appreciated as it deserved. He placed his fingers on his throat now, and let his tongue protrude, to describe the process of strangulation.

Ralph drew back in horror. It is one thing to entertain the idea of a crime hypothetically, and even to incite to the deed. The mind busies itself in contemplating the results, and the act appears but a circumstance, a necessary one perhaps, but one on which it is unnecessary to dwell. It is another thing to

confront the deed after it has been done, and
can no longer be overlooked, when it has
become a realized infamy, withering and dwin-
dling the profits and results into worthless
Dead Sea fruit. The bloodhound will pursue
its prey for days together, eager to pull him
down and bury its fangs in his flesh, but if in
the heat of the chase it should encounter
blood, there is an end, the scent is lost, the
hunt ended. And so was Ralph staggered at
what he heard. This child's life had stood in
his way, and he had striven to set it aside.
But to think that it had been murdered, and
that his was the finger which touched the
spring and set the murderous machine in motion! No! He *would* not think it. It was
horrible. The instrument, the over-zealous
instrument which had done too much, must
shoulder the responsibility of his own deed;
and, for himself, he would no longer compro-
mise his respectability by having dealings
with such a ruffian, now that it had become
quite safe to break with him. The blood of
the little innocent seemed crying out of the
ground for vengeance, and at least he would
wash his hands of the murderer, and not a
cent of blood-money should the homicide
receive from him. A virtuous glow diffused
itself through Ralph's pulses as these

thoughts passed through his mind in a space far shorter than it takes to write or read them ; indeed there had been little more than the ordinary conversational pause between Paul's last grunt of assent and pantomimic signs, and Ralph's reply as he now looked him squarely in the face with a frown of the severest virtue, and a demeanour of dignified rebuke which an ignorant onlooker might have hoped would not be lost on the poor untaught son of the wilderness.

" And you have been drawing money from me for that child's support all these years ! " He grew indignant as he thought how he had been imposed upon ; and Paul, quenched the moment before, and astonished at his demeanour, began to pluck up heart again, and the dawn of a smile at his own cleverness began to re-appear on his wooden visage ; but it faded again as Ralph proceeded :

" Do you know that what you have been accusing yourself of is a hanging offence ? A cruel, cowardly murder of a helpless infant ? But I will not be made accessory after the fact ! I am done with you, Paul !—Go !— Do you hear me ? Git ! "

Paul looked in his face amazed. What had he meant then when he promised him money to bring news of the child's death ? He

was about to speak, but Ralph stopped him
before, in his stupefaction, he could find words.

" Go ! I say.   And never let me see you
again.   Or——!   You can guess yourself
what will happen."

Confused, crestfallen and crushed, Paul
withdrew.   A new view of the inscrutable
ways of the great white man had been given
him.   He could only draw a great breath in
his helplessness and go his way.   The white
folks were too much for him, that was the one
idea which penetrated his darkened mind.
They would make use of him when they
wanted him, and then cast him aside ; but
for the future he promised himself to keep
out of their way.

Ralph coughed and drew on his gloves, not
ill-pleased, at the last, at the turn which affairs
had taken, and hurried off to catch the afternoon train for St. Euphrase, where his family
were spending the summer at a smart new villa
which he had built a year or two before.

# CHAPTER XI.

RALPH HERKIMER reached the station as the train was about to start. M. Rouget was in the act of assisting his wife and daughter into the parlour car, and Ralph sprang in after him just as the train moved from the platform. M. Rouget owned the seigniory of La Hache, on the outskirts of St. Euphrase, an outlying fragment of which Ralph had purchased and built upon, hoping that with the other products of the soil there would spring up an intimacy with the Rouget family, and thereby an entrance to that French circle which so few English-speaking Canadians ever penetrate. Not that that circle is more wealthy, or of necessity more cultured than others on the great American continent ; but language, religion, and customs make it less accessible and more exclusive, and therefore, like other things difficult, both desirable and distinguished. A certain prescriptive precedence, too, naturally attaches to the first comers everywhere, if only they are strong ʻenough to enforce it; and it must be remembered that these Lower Canada seigniors represent the earliest settlers, and as a body are the only approach to a landed aristocracy in North America. North America, it is true, is the chosen home of democracy and equality; but democratic equality— what is it? Does it not mean, my brother, that you are on no pretext whatever to claim any sort of betterness over *me*, while *I*, if I can secure distinction or superiority am to be protected in the enjoyment of my acquisition; for is it not a free and a law-abiding country that we live in? Witness the army of the decorated in democratic France! or the shoals of colonels, generals, and judges in the United States. Such is democracy. *You* must have nothing which I have not, but *I* may take whatever I can lay my hands on; and you, sir, are to bow down to me for having it. It is the autocrat's crown cut up in slices, and placed on the head of every one self-asserting enough to wear his fraction.

Ralph had made money—secured a substantial hunch of the bread of subsistence, and now he was minded to butter it with all the social distinctions and advantages he could attain to. M. Rouget passed up the car before him, preceded by madame and the demoiselle, his daughter. These ladies had not called upon Ralph's wife on her coming to reside in the neighbourhood ; but then Martha, as he told himself, though a worthy creature, and one who had made him an excellent wife in his day of small things, was scarcely equal to the promotion which had overtaken her. She was undeniably diffident and undistinguished ; perhaps even dowdy, he added with a sigh, as the fresh crisp dresses of the French ladies, befringed, bebugled, and "relieved" with streamers of lace and ribbon, swam on in front of him. He would claim his neighbour's acquaintance, he thought, who doubtless would introduce him to his family; and then he doubted not he should make himself so plea- sant that the ladies would re-consider their previous reserve and call on Martha forth- with. Already he saw himself at La Hache, invited to meet Monseigneur the Archbishop and the Honourable the Minister of Drainage and Irrigation, whom after that, if he were but civil, he should feel bound to support at future elections, though hitherto he had voted *rouge*.

So quick is thought, all this and more had flashed through his mind, illustrated with *vig- nettes* of gracious smiling ladies and gesticu-

lating Frenchmen—the prismatic glintings
of a snob's beatific vision—and he had not
yet reached the middle of the car. M. Rouget
was walking on before. Another step and he
would overtake him. Already his hand was
raised to touch the seignior's arm, when, hsh!
—the prod of a parasol point dexterously
planted in the small of his back made him
start, exclaim, stop, and turn round.

In the corner of a sofa he had passed, a
wizened little woman, somewhat dusty and
tumbled was smiling, to him from under the
frizzes of her false front, wide-mouthedly
smiling, till every gold pin in her best set of
teeth shone in the slanting sunbeams of the
afternoon. She held out a clawlike hand in a
cotton glove, by way of welcome, making room
on the sofa beside her, and dropping the parasol
point, as the wild Indian lays down his toma-
hawk in sign of amity.

"Judy!" said Ralph in some disgust; but
while he spoke he saw the Rouget party seat
themselves with some friends, and recognized
that the opportunity for his little *coup* was
past, so he recovered himself and dropped into
the place so effusively offered.

"And how come *you* to be here, ma'am?
The general car does not seem over-crowded.
If the treasurer of the diocesan fund were to

see you travelling in parlour cars, he would doubt the need of that augmentation we have been petitioning for."

"It would be just like him if he did. He is mean enough for anything in the way of prying into the private affairs of the rural clergy. I wonder how he would like it himself? Still, there *are* a few whose goings on he might inquire into more closely. But he has favourites. I wish Synod would make a change."

"But they will say *you* are a favourite if you travel in this regardlessly extravagant way."

"Let them, if they dare! But there is no fear of that. They cannot but know that on the five hundred dollars of stipend they allow Mr. Bunce, a clergyman's family cannot travel at all, except on foot; and even that takes more shoe leather than they can afford. They understand perfectly well, that, but for my little income, Mr. Bunce could not have afforded to accept the parish of St. Euphrase at all—a fact which is no credit to our church. And I think, Ralph, it would have been more respectful to Mr. Bunce, and kinder to me, if you had not alluded to our pecuniary circumstances. We cannot all be brokers, you must remember."

"Beg pardon, Judy. No offence. And you remind me that I have not yet inquired after the health of my respected uncle," he added with an impertinent laugh. "I hope he is well."

Ralph's acquisition of an uncle on his Aunt Judith's marriage was rather an ancient ground of amusement by this time, for the marriage had taken place years before; but the idea of his maiden aunt created a wife, and the cleric, his junior, transformed into his uncle, was a perennial joke, from which time and familiarity could not rub the point. His other uncle, Gerald, had been one to make a nephew quail; and that this mild, shaven, unwealthy, and, so far, youthful parson should have stepped into the redoubtable title, was inexhaustibly droll. It is notable how long the same quip and jest will serve to tickle the busy man engrossed in material interests; but in this case there was the excuse that the Bunces really were an oddly-assorted pair. A stranger could not but have inquired how they had come to marry each other—she, so mature, he, with his drab-coloured hair and round smooth cheeks. "Cherubical," his bride had called the cheeks to her brides-maid in a moment of enthusiasm and confidence ; but they were too loose and pasty to deserve the title, or if not, the cherub must have been out of health—cloyed with ambrosia perhaps, or too much nectar, in the Elysian Fields.

Judith herself had rejuvenated, or brightened, perhaps, since we saw her first, with hair and clothing severely plain, and a look of reproving superiority to all things pleasant. She was an old young woman in those days, and now she was a young old one. Then, leanness and the tight-drawn skin prevented the crows' feet round the eyes from being strongly marked, and the low-toned colouring harmonized in its way with the grizzling of the hair ; now, with some gain of adipose tissue, and the relaxed tension incident to a mind relieved from the imaginary reproach of spinsterhood, the lines and creases showed quite clearly, like ripple marks on the sand left by the ebbing waves of time. The hair, too, with its faded browns sympathizing with the greyness of the flesh tints was changed ; for now the lady shone in a new capillary outfit, and seemingly, when buying it, she had chosen to revert to the livelier colouring of her youth. The "front," "bang," "fringe," or whatever she may have called it, was of a cheerful gingerbread hue, which quenched any lingering lustre of the eye, or aspiration toward pinkness in the cheek, and gave her somewhat the look of a mummy, which, after ages wasted in darkness, comes forth again to taste the happiness of life, and the warmth of the upper world.

The love tale of these two had no doubt been as thrilling an idyl to themselves as that of any pair of nightingales in all Arcadia, but it appeared rather a drab-coloured romance, or, better, no romance at all, to their friends, who opened their eyes in blank amaze when the project of marriage was announced, and vowed the strangely-assorted couple had lost their wits. Judith, the severely Protestant virgin of St. Silas, to the High Church—the very high—curate of St. Wittikind's! It seemed incredible. It was true that for some time she had visited a good deal among the poor of St. Wittikind's parish, frequented its schools, guilds and sisterhoods, where things were conducted not precisely as the good people of St. Silas thought best; but still that was "Church work," and as she continued to distribute tracts as copiously as ever in the Catholic neighbourhood selected by the St. Silas' ladies as their experimental farm of controversy, they had agreed to regard the vagary as only showing great breadth of view, and a largely comprehensive charity, which they hoped would lead to reciprocity, and bring some darkling wanderer from the other pen to their own better-lighted fold.

The reality of the case was far otherwise. Miss Judith had a leisure and energy ravenous of occupation, and which would not be filled up, and appeased with fancy-work, and dispensing printed leaves to French people who could not understand what she said. These are pleasing occupations, but they grow monotonous after a time. She had tried improving her mind, too, a good work, but it postulates a mind capable of being improved by printed matter, and the minds of many who have done the world's work, and done it well, have not been of that kind. Miss Judith's mind was practical rather than contemplative, and her studies did not go great lengths, while nature had blessed her with a sustaining self-content. When her book wearied her she laid it down and sought some other occupation—somebody else to improve, when her own mind had had enough of it. Her sister Susan declined her offices, knowing the teacher too well to set much

store by the lessons, and therefore she had
to carry her instructions farther afield.

Such is the sad lot of spinsterhood
in modern life, when woman misses her
natural vocation of house-mother, and
fortune exempts her from the need to
earn her living. The instincts and traits
which society for its own entertainment
encouraged and cultivated in youth lose
their power to please when bloom and
sprightliness have vanished. Then the love
of applause and excitement so attractive in
the youthful beauty turn like famished
hounds on their forsaken mistress, and rend
her own heart when she can furnish them
no other game. She has been taught to
think highly of herself, and to claim much,
and she may have learned the world and its
lessons well, but the world has grown weary
of her, and goes its way in search of a fresher
plaything. There is tragedy in this of the
unspoken kind, but it is so common, and
it drags its course so slowly—for people do
not easily die of spinsterhood—that we fail
to note the restless gnawing of hearts and
brains condemned to inaction, and only laugh
at the *bizarrerie*, when, growing intolerable,
it breaks out into lady-doctors of divinity,
law, or physic.

When Judith made the acquaintance of the Rev. Dionysius Bunce, it was with something of the trepidation with which an explorer clambers up the side of an unknown volcano. " Could he be a Jesuit in disguise, as some people said?" she wondered, " or was he a well-meaning but uninstructed person who had lost his way, and now unwittingly was travelling the broad and flowery road, whose course is ever downward, and which leads, we all know whither?" What an achievement it would be could she lead back the wanderer, if indeed he were astray! Or if he were, as she had been taught to think, a wolf in sheep's clothing, what a privilege to unmask him and save true Protestantism from his insidious wiles!

But there was a single-minded earnestness in this young man which interested her from the first, and soon assured her he was no Jesuit; and he was so strangely willing to listen, to discuss, and even to admit that there might be much in her view of a question. This was new to Judith, whose guides hitherto, knowing all about everything, had tolerated no differences of opinion, and had shown her the path of orthodoxy laid down with square and compass from which no one must venture to diverge under pain of running up against some text of Scripture, set like a curbstone by the wayside, to the peril of unwary wheels meandering off the track. Dionysius was self-denying in his charity, too. He would give his dinner to the poor any day, instead of dining first and bestowing the leavings, as is more usual; and self-denial is a virtue which enthusiastic women delight in. Enthusiasm is catching, and when it has caught, it makes scattered units run together and cohere like drops of quicksilver. Judith had caught it from him as had the members of his guilds; and they worked away with a happy feeling of earnestness which made things very pleasant, and over-rode all misgivings as to whether the dance were worth the candle, or at least as to the usefulness or wisdom of what they were about.

Judith was drawn by the fervour of St. Wittikind's curate into visiting his poor, and even decorating his sanctuary—a Low Church lady actually embroidering crosses and polemical symbols!—and yet in her new frame of mind it did not occur to her she had at first discussed with disapproval the use of papistical emblems. He had treated her view with every respect while differing from it, and then had talked round the point to the other side, and shown the amiable and pious feeling in which such things may be done when looked at the other way, till Judith, won by his toleration, could not but be tolerant too, and actually joined in the work.

It must have been this mixture of docility and independence which won on Dionysius, and recalled the sacred feelings with which in his boyhood he had regarded a venerable aunt and a saintly mother both deceased. He was a young man of a pre-eminently earnest cast of mind, which turned churchwards. He greatly admired and fain would have copied the saints and heroes of early times. Had the Church of Canada kept a wilderness for retiring into, like the Thebæid of antiquity, he would have turned hermit; or had there been some real genuine pagans within its confines he would have been a missionary; but the Indian of the North-West, part horse-thief, part fur-trader, and altogether in-different, offers no opening to aspirants to the rank of martyr or confessor ; so he was forced to do like the rest, and stay at home.

He did what he could in St. Wittikind's, but it was discouraging work. The men there were mostly wealthy, and all en-grossed in business. They could not be induced to attend either daily matins or evensong, and though scrupulously polite when he approached them, were sure to have an important appointment somewhere, and forced to hurry away. The young ladies of course were ready, nay charmed, to attend matins or anything else, provided the hour was reasonable and there had been no ball overnight. Evensong he found unpopular with them, as interfering with " home duties," to wit afternoon tea; but they were eager for "Church work," at least in the shape of elaborate embroideries in gold thread and ecclesiastical patterns. If Dionysius would have interested himself in croquet or lawn tennis, or if he would have nourished a taste for music of a form less severe than Gregorians, he would have come to have influence; but the young man at that stage of his growth was too single-minded to have any mistress but Religion; and Mrs. Silvertongue, his rector's worldly-minded wife, was heard to compare him to a shaggy young Baptist broke loose from the desert, when Judith rushed to the rescue by declaring that he seemed to be a very sound Churchman indeed, and everybody laughed at both the ladies.

As years went on, the intimacy grew closer. Judith found it delightful to be busy and of importance—to be authorized to interfere with people too poor to dare resent it; telling them what they must do, scolding and physicking them as seemed best, and really being kind, though in a provoking way; consulting with a clergyman, talking and being listened to by a gentleman with interest and respect. It was so very long ago since any gentleman had shown interest in her conversation, or anything but weariness, and now this ordained pastor sometimes even consulted her. It made her feel that she was not yet all of the past, that there was something to live for still, and afforded some of the old time satisfaction in being minded by one of the stronger sex, mixed at once with the reverence she owed a spiritual guide, and motherly interest in one so much her junior.

Dionysius, too, grew attached, though not precisely in the same way as if she had been twenty years younger. He was so good a young man, and so shy, that he failed, perhaps, to fill all the social uses of a curate, and grew somewhat out of intimacy with the younger ladies of his cure, who, though they saw him daily at matins, had learned not to look for his presence at garden parties and afternoon teas. Judith listened to him with so ardent an interest that he forgot his diffidence and reserve in conversing with her, and grew even eloquent at times, as he knew by the admiring

reverence in her face; and then, in the gratification of appreciated merit, he would forget
the disparity in their ages, and hail her as a
sister spirit travelling the same heavenward
road with himself. And so they continued
to fare on together in amity and trust, the
brother uttering words of wisdom, the sister
accepting them humbly, and ignorant that
they were leading her far from the truth
according to St. Silas, where with her sister
on Sundays she still went to church; for
Judith's theological mind was of the emotional
not the argumentative sort; though she loved
to use the party catch-words, and believed
she set great store by them, they conveyed
to her no clearly defined ideas. Warmth
was what she longed for, and friendship, and
these she drew most readily from the curate
of St. Wittikind.

The intimacy between the two might have
gone on for ever unchanged, but at length
Dionysius fell ill, and then the crisis in their
friendship and their lives arrived. Judith
called regularly at her friend's lodging to
inquire for his health. By-and-by she had
messages to carry him from his poor, she sat
down by his bedside and conversed, and he
declared himself so much refreshed by her visit
that it would have been inhuman if she had

not called again. She did call again, and again ;
and by-and-by she fell into the way of bringing jellies and little dainties to tempt the sick
man's appetite.  One day as he was dining on
a warm and greasy broth, misnamed beef tea,
he laid it down scarce tasted on her entrance,
and with manifest disrelish pushed it away.
Judith peered and sniffed at the ungrateful
preparation, and pressed him to try her jelly
instead.  " I know how beef-tea should be
made, and I shall bring your landlady a
supply, and then she will only have to warm
a little from time to time as you want it."

The next day Judith arrived, carrying
upstairs with difficulty a large stone jar in a
basket.  In the study, which was also the
ante-chamber to the sick-room, she en-
countered the landlady coming out.  Mrs.
McQuirter looked her full in the face, flushing
indignantly and eyeing with a sniff and a toss
of the head the jar which Judith was lifting
with difficulty to the table.

" Good morning, Mrs. McQuirter," said
Judith in her most conciliatory manner.

" Morning, miss," replied the other with
a side-long glance which was far from friendly.

" How do you think Mr. Bunce is to-day,
Mrs. McQuirter ? "

" Guess you're going in, miss, and will see

for yourself; so there's no good me telling you. You'd be sure to think you knew a deal better," and she sailed towards the door in her grandest style ; then turning as if an idea had struck her, and as if fearing that she had not already been sufficiently provoking, she added :

"Say, miss! Is that sleigh as brought you and your basket still at the door? We've a deal of old crockery here as don't belong to us, and we'd be right glad to be rid on. Odd bowls, and plates, and chipped jelly glasses as don't match our sets, and make me feel kind o' mean when neighbours come in at dish-washing time with their 'Laws, Mrs. McQuirter, now ! and where in goodness did you ever pick up all them cracked dishes ?' If you're agreeable, I will just get 'em all together and send them back by the carman before they get broke, for it 'ud cost more than the valy of all the messes they brought here to replace 'em with new."

Judith felt indignant, and coloured deeply, but as to reply in kind would have been to raise a dragon in the path to her friend's bedside, she restrained herself, and merely answered : "By all means, Mrs. McQuirter. Kindly help me to lift this jar out of the basket, and then you can take it."

" And what may you be bringing here in your large crock, miss?" asked the landlady contemptuously. It seemed so impossible to irritate this old maid into the scolding match she thirsted for, that she was growing to despise as well as detest her.

" This is some beef-tea—a most excellent form in which to give nourishment to invalids like Mr. Bunce."

" Beef-tea, indeed! It's more like half-melted glue to look at. Ugh!"

" Quite natural in you to say so, Mrs. McQuirter. So few people know what beef-tea really should be like. It is the strength of the stock, which has jellied in cooling, that gives it the appearance you allude to. If you will just warm a cupful in a saucepan as it is wanted, without letting it boil, you will find it delicious. Try a little of it yourself, I know you will like it."

" Not me! And do you know, miss, how many large knuckles of beef I have boiled into tea in the last ten days? And scarce a drop has he let pass his lips! All clean gone to waste. I don't hold with beef-tea for Mr. Bunce no ways. He seems to hate it like pizen."

" I am not surprised at his having refused the decoction I saw sent up to him yesterday,"

13—2

said Judith with a relish. It seemed that notwithstanding her forbearance she was to have an innings, and she meant to use it in truly Christian fashion; not to exult openly, but to rub any blistering truth which came to hand well into the bone. "In making beef-tea all fat is carefully removed, and the meat is then placed in a jar with salt and cold water, near the fire, where it must stand for hours without boiling or even simmering. Now, really, Mrs. McQuirter," and she dipped a teaspoon in the jar, "just taste how good it is! If you will warm a cup or so of it two or three times a day I am confident you will have no difficulty in getting Mr. Bunce to drink it."

"I think I see me trying it, miss! And it shows your assurance to be evening me to the like. You are but a young lady yet, so to say, though you were born ten years before myself, I guess, as am the mother of six—leastways you are but an old maid, when all is said, and to take upon you to tell *me* how to make beef-tea! Me, as am the mother of six, and has buried a good husband. And many a bowl of my beef-tea the poor man drank, and him lying on the very feather bed where the parson lies now."

"And he died, Mrs. McQuirter? I am not

surprised," said Miss Judith, thinking more of her argument and less of conciliation as the talk went on. "I observed the mixture yesterday when Mr. Bunce was unable to swallow it—a mere mixture of grease and warm water. Do you not know that at boiling point albumen coagulates, and becomes insoluble, like the white of a hard-boiled egg? You would not expect the water you boil eggs in to be very nourishing? Your beef-tea is just like that, and if your late husband's dietary contained no more nourishing items, I cannot wonder that he did not survive."

"You owdacious old maid, you! How daar you? To insinniwate that me as has fairly slaved for my man and his children had a hand to his taking off. But I'll have the law of you, I will! and I take Mr. Bunce in there as must have heard ye, if he's awake yet, to witness that you said it. Me, the mother of six, to be insulted and put upon by an old thing as never was able to get married at all! And it shows the men's good sense, that same. And here you come with your broths and your messes after my poor young gentleman, as is laid on the broad of his back, and too sick to run away from you like the rest. And it's a disgrace to your sect, you are, miss! for all your silk, and your sealskin,

and me but a poor lone widdy with a quiet
lodger—to be coming here at all hours acourt-
ing a gentleman as don't want you—you that
are old enough to be his grandmother and
should be at home making your soul, for
your change as must come before long,
'stead of running that shameless after the men
to make them marry you."

"Oh!" was all that Judith could utter,
throwing up her black gloved hands to the
ceiling and then dropping in a heap on a stool
in the corner and burying her face in her
handkerchief. The wordy hurricane had
fallen on the flower—an elderflower—and
beaten it down and crushed it; and there she
cowered in her confusion, convulsed with
sobs, while the hurricane whistled but the more
wildly in its triumph, and would fain have
scattered and dispersed the ruin it had already
made.

"And well may you hide your face after
sich ongoings! and it don't become one as
sets up for quality to have done the like; to
be coming here a worritting of a poor young
gentleman to marry her, as it's quite oncertain
if he will see the light of next week! Or is it
that you think you will make the people say
he has treated you bad if he don't, after you
coming here so often? But the people knows

better, miss! and they say you're too old for
him ; and that you've been worritting around
him that long, it's a fair amazement between
his patience and your perseverance whatever
comes of it. The very rector of the parish
takes notice on it, and the rector's lady says
its shameless the way you go on to make him
marry you!"

"Silence, Mrs. McQuirter! with your bad
and cruel tongue."

Mrs. McQuirter turned and stood aghast.
The door of the sleeping-room had opened
without noise, and framed in the opening
stood Dionysius, like the picture of his
canonized namesake stepped out of some
Gothic window. One arm was thrust into the
sleeve of a purple dressing-gown which was
wrapped about him, leaving exposed his chest
and other arm clothed in their snowwhite
sleeping gear. Excitement caused by the
altercation he must have overheard, and the
exertion of rising had brought a feverish
flush to his cheeks, burning into hectic spots
amid the pallor of illness, and there was a
lustre in his eye, which could the world
have seen, it would have reconsidered its
judgment of his appearance as ordinary and
commonplace.

"How dare you address my kind visitor—

my friend—in the wicked words I have heard
you use?"

Mrs. McQuirter was taken aback; but
being now, to use her own phrase, "in for it,"
as having sinned beyond forgiveness, and sure
to lose her lodger, it seemed best to retreat in
good order, and show neither fear nor remorse.

"What a lone widdy like me says, Mr.
Bunce, ain't of no 'count to a gentleman
like you, sir, and I have always done my very
best to make you comfortable, so my mind's
easy. It's what the rector's lady says, and the
quality in your church, and if you like to have
them speaking that way of you and that—that
female there, as is ashamed to look an honest
woman in the face, 'taint no affairs of mine."

Judith felt as if she would gladly die, and
sank from the stool to the carpet in a collapsed
heap. If the ground would have opened
and swallowed her, how thankful she would
have been; but it did not, and she could but
bury her face deeper in her lap.

"The lady you have presumed to scandalize
so shamefully," the curate resumed, "has called
here at my earnest request. If I could induce
her to come more frequently she would be
even more welcome; and in case you should
still have any doubts, let me tell you plainly
that if this lady would condescend to accept

me, there is no one I would so gladly make
my wife. Now! I have said all that can
possibly interest you. Leave the room instantly, and close the door."

The door closed behind Mrs. McQuirter and
the two were left together. Judith's confusion was too great to permit her to lift her
head, but there was a tremor of expectancy
in the heap of silk and sealskin into which she
had collapsed, which made itself felt in the
surrounding air. She had ceased to sob, and
became all ear. Even the silk of her gown,
though she was crouched so close that to draw
breath without a movement seemed impossible,
forbore to rustle.

Dionysius stood still in his white and purple
like a Gothic saint, but less erect now that
the impulse of battle had spent itself. He
stood a committed man, yet a man who has
not yet spoken, shivering on the brink of the
proposal which he has bound himself to
make. You remember the feeling, my married
friend, when the words grew too unwieldy to
articulate, and there was a pause. The leading up to the grand climax had been achieved,
the lady and the universe were waiting, the
very next word must be the word of fate, and
you were not dreaming of drawing back, but
still it lingered; and oh! the effort it took to

launch that ill-formed sentence! Dionysius stood, and his strength was waning. Before him there was the prostrate heap of clothing which waited but made no sign, and the air around was still and listening. The very fire forgot to blaze and crackle, and looked at him silently in red unblinking expectation. Only the clock on the mantelpiece went on unmoved, counting the fleeting seconds as they sped with dispassionate calmness. They were slipping away, and so too was his strength, and yet he had not spoken.

"Judith," he said at last with a great effort; but when he had so far found his voice the words came easier.

"Judith, my fr——Judith!" and he went and laid a tremulous hand upon her shoulder. "You have heard the words I spoke to Mrs. McQuirter. Will you forgive me that I should thus have declared myself in the presence of a stranger before having spoken to yourself. Believe me, dear, it was from no disrespect, no lack of appreciation; but you know how we have been with each other. Our close fellowship in the higher life may have made us forgetful of mere earthly relations, but we must remedy that now. This foolish woman, with her idle tongue, has spoken words of more wisdom than she knew, and if we are to be companions on the heavenward way, is it not well that our earthly paths should be united ? "

A thrill ran all through Judith's frame. He felt her tremble beneath his hand, but still she did not lift her head.

"Judith, my own dear, you must marry me! It is necessary for your good name. If that is not enough to move you, it is necessary for mine. I will not have them say that I could trifle with a woman's regard. Though what care we, either you or I, for people's idle talk ? Have we not been walking hand-in-hand, each helping and supporting the other to live aright ? And has not our companionship been for good to both ? Let us marry, Judith! and silence babbling tongues. It will be best so. Look up, my friend, and answer. And yet, Judith, I must own it, I am poor. I have nothing but the stipend of my curacy ; and when the poor, my brothers, have had their share, and my yearly bills are paid, there is nothing over. Not a cent. It will explain to you how I never came to think of marriage before."

Then Judith raised her face suffused with blushes, and lighted with a happy eager look which had not been seen there before in twenty years ; and under the transfiguring influence of an unexpected joy, she looked for the moment almost beautiful. So, when the fogs and rain of autumn have spent their strength, and the frosts of winter still linger in their coming, there fall halcyon days, when nature, not yet stripped bare of flower and foliage, blooms out again in her Indian summer. The trees are hung with wreaths of gold-bright leaves, or garlanded with crimson, the sod renewed by rains after the summer scorchings, is green with a greenness unseen at other times ; the garden is still cheered by marigolds and asters, larkspur and phlox, and the sky and the waters have a sunny blueness, shining but the brighter for the smoky grey which conceals the distance—the distance which harbours winter, tempest, rain, too soon to be let loose.

A tear was quivering on Judith's eyelash. A happy sob gave a tremor to her voice when she tried to speak.

" Dionysius. And do you mean it ? Marry —marry me ! But it is only your gentlemanly feeling which will not have me talked about. I dare not take you at your word, however— however much—I might——" and her colour deepened, and the drops rained down, and again she hid her face.

" Indeed, it is not so, Judith. You may indeed believe me—if only you will have it so.

And we have been so much to each other—
and now we must be nothing any more, unless
you will consent to marry."

Judith moved as if trying to gain her feet,
and Dionysius took her hand to lend assistance,
and so it came about that they stood with
their arms entwined. Judith's head dropped
on the curate's shoulder, and felt as if it would
gladly linger there for ever. And he, the lady
clinging and half-supported in his arms, had a
vague sense of heroic worth and power as
man; standing thus before the universe,
lord of another life besides his own; and
many other feelings, surging and confused,
which would not lend themselves to words.
And little more was said, though much was
understood and agreed between them; and
by-and-by the striking of the clock recalled
them to common life, and both sat down.
Then Dionysius, exhausted with excitement,
grew faint and returned to his room.

Judith lingered till she was assured that the
faintness was wearing off, and then she stole
softly downstairs on her way home. Softly as
she stepped, however, she was overheard, and
ere she could reach the door, Mrs. McQuirter
stood before her blocking the way; but it was
Mrs. McQuirter in a different part from the
one she had played so lately. Then, she was

the dragon landlady ready to devour an intrusive and defenceless spinster, now she was the lone widow, the mother of six. One little toddler held on to her gown, she led another by the hand, while her other hand held a napkin saturated with the moisture which ran from her streaming eyes and bedewed her face.

"Oh, miss!" she cried with a sob, and the little ones piped a small chorus of sympathy, "I was wishful to speak to you as you went out, to make it up with you for what I said upstairs. And I'm free to confess, miss, it was not my place to speak the way I did. But I'm hot by nature, miss, and when once I begin, my tongue runs clean away from me. But I bear no malice, miss, as John McQuirter often said. 'She bears no malice,' he'd say, and them's his very words."

"It is of no consequence, Mrs. McQuirter; I'm willing to overlook," and Judith endeavoured to slide past in the narrow hallway, but the little ones, with faces damp and sticky, and threatening damage to any article of apparel which might rub against them in passing, blocked the way.

"And it's good of you to say so much, miss; and it does credit to Mr. Bunce's choice. And oh, Miss! you'll remember, will you not?

I'm a lone widdy, and the mother of six! And it's hoping you'll have a fine family of your own some day," which made Judith blush. "And you won't be for allowing Mr. Bunce to change his lodging, and all along of a few thoughtless words, as I'm truly sorry for the saying on. You won't now? Will'e, miss? Like a dear."

"I have told you, already, Mrs. McQuirter, I shall overlook the offence. Mr. Bunce is too ill to think of moving. He feels quite faint after the disturbance you caused him, and he needs nourishment. You had better warm him a cupful of that beef-tea I brought. Warm it in a saucepan, but don't let it boil; and send up a few sippets of dry toast along with it. The sooner you can let him have it the better." And having prescribed this penance to the spirit-broken mother of six, she got away.

It was near the end of Lent before the secret of the engagement was divulged, though the wedding was to be immediately after Easter; but then a storm of ridicule arose which could not but offend those most interested. Judith's own family were as provokingly sarcastic as any one in the churches of St. Silas or St. Wittikind, and that is saying much. It became clear to the young couple that they must leave the city; so Dionysius resigned his curacy and accepted the small missionary parish of St. Euphrase. The emoluments there were less than he had enjoyed in the city, but his wife was possessed of a modest competency, on which in that sequestered place, they contrived to live in comfort and respect.

If the taste in which Judith had endeavoured to rejuvenate her appearance was doubtful, the acquisition of a spouse had still had the best influence in softening and sweetening her nature, and her gratitude and devotion to the man who had looked on her in her loneliness were pleasant to see. For him, it was only after marriage and the worship which it brought him at his own fireside, that it began to dawn on Mr. Bunce what a very superior man he must surely be, and he felt beholden to his helpmate for making the discovery. So Mahomet no doubt, felt to the elderly Kadijah, his first wife, the earliest of his converts, and the first to recognize him as a prophet. In after years he married women younger and more beautiful, but none ever held a place so high in his affection as the wealthy widow who had married him in his poverty and youth.

# CHAPTER XII.

## A GARDEN TEA.

IT was on the same afternoon as that referred
to, previous to the long digression in the last
chapter, but perhaps a trifle earlier, though
the torrid glare of mid-day had passed, and
the cool shadows below the trees had begun
to creep eastward on the shaven lawn. The
air was full of warmth and sunshine, with just
stir enough to move the aspen leaves upon
the tree, and scatter more faint and widely
the scent of roses beyond the alleys, where
it hung in drowsy sweetness, mingling with
the droning of bees and inviting to mid-day
sleep, that crowning deliciousness of summer
weather.

The Misses Stanley were in their grounds,
and they had friends. They were in their
grounds, that is to say in a shady corner of the
lawn by the house, where three or four grand
hemlocks, survivors of the forest, spread out
umbrageous arms over a glimmering arcade of

gloom, where never sunbeam stole, and the
shady air was fresh with the fragrant breath
of resins drawn from the upper branches
by the sun. There, lounging on cane chairs
and garden seats, they plied their fans calmly,
and chatted, but not too much or loud, in
sociable repose. It was early in July, when
everything is green and fresh and vigorous—
bud, bloom, and spray instinct with brimming
life, and not a yellowing leaf to tell of memories
or regret, all hope and promise and delight in
the flowery present and the fruitful days to
come. Great butterflies were tumbling in the
brightness, and there was a low continuous
murmur in the grass from the thousand living
things too small to be separately or distinctly
heard ; and ever and anon from around the
banks of shrubs would come the gurgling
laughter of youthful voices, so lightsome in
its freedom from care and adult emotion.

There were six of them, those youthful
ones, whose merry voices disturbed the slum-
brous heat, walking or running, heedless alike
of shade and sunshine, their hands full of
roses.  Muriel was one of them, the ladies'
niece, and Tilly Martindale, Miss Matilda's god-
daughter, and Betsey Bunce, a niece of the
rector, and so a sort of cousin to the family.
There was Gerald Herkimer, Ralph's only

child, whose mother Martha was sitting with the ladies in the shade, and Randolph Jordan, the son of Matilda's friend Amelia who was sitting by her at that moment. And, last, there was Pierre Bruneau, a black-eyed *habitant* boy, the son of Jean, who managed the farm. He had been working in the garden, and seeing Muriel, had found some small service to render her, and had lingered near, unconscious of the sidelong glances of her companions. She had given him her flowers to carry and bade him bring them to the house, and he, intoxicated with their fragrance, or rather, perhaps, at being permitted to carry them for his mistress when the young gentlemen were by, joined gaily in the general laughter, and even ventured to put in a jest in his queer French-English, to the amusement and placation of the not over-well pleased company.

They were all between fifteen and seventeen years old, all except Muriel. Muriel was eleven, and all the promise of her babyhood, which had dropped so unexpectedly into the ladies' arms, had been more than fulfilled. The roses and the butterflies were pale dim things beside her, as she skipped among the rest, her long hair shining like threads of gold where it caught the light, and melting into a warm shadow beneath the

14—2

leaf of her spreading garden-hat, from beneath whose brim there shone a pair of eyes luminous in their glee and innocency, penetrating without sharpness and soft without being dull ; lips short, red, and parted, displaying teeth small, regular, well apart, like a string of evenly-assorted pearls.

The fête was hers—her birthday it was called —and in reality it was the anniversary of her appearance in her present life, on the night after the thunderstorm, when the ladies had found her on their doorsteps. Penelope, prudent and timid, would rather have left the day unmarked, in case talk should arise ; but Matilda, emboldened by success in her plan of adoption, insisted that fears were now idle, "that their darling must keep her birthday like other children, and that it would be unthankful to the good Providence who had sent the little one to brighten their humdrum lives, if they kept the feast on any other day. Besides, what was there to fear ? Every servant in the house had been changed over and over in the ten years which had intervened since then ; even Smithers the nurse, who had stayed the longest, was gone these three years, and she had not only been paid to hold her tongue, but was too fond of the child to let slip a word which could injure her. Only Bruneau and his family remained about the place, and they were such quiet and respectful *habitants* they would not babble; and even if they would, who could understand them? The servants did not understand French, and Jean's and his wife's English was so awkward and hard to come, they never spoke to any of them if it could be avoided. There was the boy Pierre, to be sure, " But remember, sister, how respectful he has always been, even when, years ago, we used to send for him to come and play with Muriel; and now that he has grown big and able to work, he seems to pay far more attention to the orders she gives him than to any of ours." So Penelope shrugged her shoulders with a sigh, as she always did in the end when Matilda was " positive," and yielded the point.

" What a pretty, graceful child Muriel is," said Mrs. Martindale, Tilly's mother, a widow. They had come from Montreal for the fête.

" Yes, indeed," said Mrs. Jordan, " she will make a sensation in Montreal when you bring her out, Matilda; but that is some years in the future yet. The other girls had better make haste and arrange themselves before she appears," and she glanced at Mrs. Martindale, which was gratuitously unkind, seeing that

Tilly, being only fifteen, would not appear in the world for two winters to come, and she promised to be a remarkably fine girl, and in quite a different style. But then her boy Randolph had been essaying to pipe his first small note for ladies' ears in those of the damsel, and she, though not yet out, was grown woman enough to desiderate whiskers or a moustache in an admirer, and to scorn with youth's uncompromising freedom the advances of a callow swain of her own tender years. Ten years later, how different her views will be! But so, in ten years' time, will his be too—and the gentleman will have the pull then, as much as the lady has it now. Wherefore, my dear Mrs. Amelia, you might very well have forborne to resent the seeming slight upon your boy! But women are such partisans, especially the good ones; and she who is not, even if she be half a philosopher, is but half a woman—and not the best half either.

And now the creaking of the entrance gate was heard, and the crunching of wheels on the gravel; and presently from among the clumps of shrubbery which screened them from the road there issued a *calèche*, the French Canadian substitute for an American buggy, high set and hung on leather straps instead of springs; and in it swung the rector and his spouse, trundling along to the front of the house.

Mrs. Jordan lifted her *pince-nez* to her eyes. "Ha! a calash! Mr. Bunce, of course. Nobody else would get into such a thing."

"Do you know, I like them, and they are very much used down at Quebec," observed Mrs. Martindale, rendered generally contradictious by the tone of the other's recent remarks.

"They make me seasick. I feel as if I were in a cradle."

"Was that the effect your cradle had, Amelia dear? You have certainly an uncommon memory to recollect so well; for surely you were in the advanced class at Mrs. Jones' when I was learning my letters."

"Quite true, Louisa," said the other, biting her lip; "but you know you were a backward child. Great talent is often slow in showing itself, you know. What a droll pair those two make, swinging up there in company—as contented as Darby and Joan carrying their eggs to market. Ah, now they are out of sight—gone round to the front door. I am told that on their wedding tour they were mistaken for mother and son—and, strange to say, the error did not put them out in the least."

"I think it nice, myself," said Penelope, " to see people so content to be happy in their own way, and so indifferent to the world's idle talk. It *is* idle talk, Amelia. When two people find each other's company desirable, are they not foolish to give it up for fear that somebody else will laugh? How much would that somebody else do to make either of them happy? And how little he *could* do. Perhaps you do not know, Amelia, that Mr. Bunce is our cousin, and therefore we feel bound to like him. At the same time he is your rector, of course, while you are living at St. Euphrase, and I admit your right to criticise him."

And here the clerical pair coming through a window from the drawing-room descried the party in the shade and joined them, which changed the conversation; at the same time the crunching gravel gave notice of other arrivals. First, a waggonette carrying Jordan, Considine and Ralph; and before these had time to alight and join the rest, a rockaway, with the family from La Hache. Mrs. Martha Herkimer, who had been enjoying the heat and the coolness and the buzz of talk in a large lounging chair, with her fan drooping listlessly in her hand, and her pose indicating enjoyment of the quiescent if not somnolent kind, roused

herself, shook out her skirts, and sat down
again bolt upright, ready to become acquainted
with the French people her husband so wished
to know, as soon as possible.

Madame Rouget led by her lord, hat in hand,
and followed by her daughter, all smiles and
sweetness, fluttered through the window to
the grass, where her hostesses met her and
exchanged salutations eked out with gesture,
in which gloves a little brighter and eyebrows
a trifle more arched than the Anglo-Saxon
pattern bore an important part. Madame's
English was not fluent; the Misses Stanley, with
the backwardness of their nation, did not venture to use French, and there was some obscurity and delay in the opening phrases,
during which M. Rouget stood benevolently
by, still uncovered and regardless of sun and
sunstroke. In time they reached the grateful
shade of the hemlocks, where the newcomers
inhaled the perfumed coolness with infinite
relish, after the glare and dust of their recent
drive; and then there came presentations of
the lately come neighbours, with profuse ex-
planations from Madame, "that her English
so *difficile* had made her delay, till she was so
*comblée* of confusions, that—— Ah, well! she
prayed the ladies to excuse;" and she smiled
very graciously, and pressed the hands of

Amelia and Martha, lisping hopes to be better acquainted; meaning, no doubt, as with Penelope and her sister, the exchange of half-yearly visits, which, in view of differences of church as well as language, was as much as could be expected. That church counted for a great deal became evident when " Mrs. Bunce, the wife of my cousin the rector," was next presented. The smile died out of Madame's face, and the *empressement* faded from her manner as she bowed more deeply than before with eyes fastened on the ground. "The *bêtise*," as she said to her daughter afterwards, " of those English! To introduce the wife of one of their married priests to me, the niece of My Lord the Archbishop!"

" But he is of their family, we must recollect, my mother," replied this judicious young person. "And perhaps they do not know of my great uncle the Archbishop. At least the ladies intended to be kind, and Monsieur Gerald Herkimaire, and Monsieur Randolphe are both *très comme il faut?*" On which Madame patted the precocious utterer of so much wisdom—she was not yet sixteen—with her fan, and laughed heartily. But this did not occur till the following morning.

Penelope was not slow to perceive that the last presentation had not been a success, and came promptly to the rescue, by asking Mrs. Bunce a question, while Matilda drew off the attention of the others by asking Mademoiselle if she would not join the young people, and leading her away, while the mother and the rest fell into conversation with the gentlemen.

The young ones by this time had sent Pierre to the house with their flowers, and were lingering on Muriel's croquet ground until Miss Martindale should persuade herself that she was not too grown up to play, a conclusion which she speedily arrived at on the appearance of the new comer, who was quite as advanced as herself and seemed eager to begin.

" How your niece is most *gracieuse*, and so prettee ! " said the Frenchwoman to Matilda when she rejoined the elders.

" Yes, indeed ! " said Mrs. Martindale, " she is one of the very nicest little girls I know ; and so clever. You should hear her play. It is more like a grown person's performance than a child's. And to think she should never have had any governess but dear Matilda here ! I call it quite remarkable."

" Ah " said Madame sympathetically. It is always a safe observation to make, especially in reply to what has not been very clearly understood, and the inflection of the voice can make it stand for so many things, that if it is only uncertain it will mean whatever the hearer likes best.

"It is a loss to society that women like you should be independent, Matilda," said Amelia. "What a governess you would have made! You need not shrug; it is a compliment, and one which very few people can claim. If you knew the troubles of governess-ridden mothers, you would understand me; so few are worth much, and those few keep one in constant dread of their growing dissatisfied and leaving, till the mother's life becomes a burden. I am so glad my family consists only of a boy, and it is Jordan's business to think what is to become of him," glancing at the croquet players.

"That young gentleman," said Madame, following the direction of the other's eyes. "*Distingué!* What joy to have one so fine son!"

Mrs. Jordan smiled her gratification and could not help glancing across at Mrs. Martindale, whose daughter's depreciation of the paragon must have ruffled her maternal plumage not a little.

"Yes," she said, "he is a dear boy—so manly and yet so affectionate," and her eyes drooped, and her voice fell, as it will when one talks of something near the heart; and there were signs—woman of the world though she was—of her maundering on upon the same sweet theme, if only there were an attentive silence.

But this Mrs. Martha's patience could not yield. She saw nothing so remarkable in the Jordan boy " for that affected French woman to make a fuss about. If it had been her Gerald now, there might have been some sense in it—with his delicate fair skin like a girl's, and his sturdy broad shoulders. It was true young Jordan had the advantage in height ; but what matters half an inch? And as to the manliness——" And again she seemed to be standing in an upper window of her town house, securely hid behind a curtain, looking down on the two boys in a tussle. How her boy tumbled the other over, let him get up and knocked him down again, and pummelled him till he had had enough. And she? Had she been a right-minded person—taken in the abstract— of course she would have interfered ; but being only a woman and a mother, and seeing it was her side which played the winning game, she merely stood and looked on. Lady lecturers and authors often tell us of the higher moral plane from which the gentle sex surveys the world's affairs, but for honest old-world delight in sheer physical force and muscular prowess, can a woman be equalled? It must be a survival from the days of savagery and marriage by capture. The learned professor's wife may expect to be led out to dinner before plain mistress, but as likely as not she is innocent of even a smattering of the " ology " on which her husband's reputation is built; but she whom good fortune has wed to a Victoria Cross knows every detail of his achievements and believes herself married to a demigod.

But this is digression. It seemed to Martha that Amelia was about to moralize aloud upon her boy, and having a kindness for her and being unwilling that she should make herself absurd, she broke the momentary silence with

" And really, Miss Matildy now "—Martha was a lady ' Noo Hampshire '—" doo tell ! Have you taught the child her letters and pothooks and some of the multiplication table all by yourself; and you not married? Well, now, I call it real smart—you might almost do for a school marm. That you might, with just taking pains—at least, if you, had begun earlier."

Ralph was standing within earshot, and it is not unlikely that he wished his wife had not spoken. She was a good soul, he well knew. She had been a beauty, and once there had seemed a quaint charm in the direct and high-pitched utterances which stole from between those coral lips. But that was years ago. The lips were withered now; it was on account of her poor health they had come to live at St. Euphrase, and only the unusual and impolite utterances remained to wound the sensibilities of polished ears— now, too, when he had become rich, and he could buy her whatever she wanted, and would have bought her some conventional refinement as gladly as her diamonds from Tiffany's. It was Matilda, however, who replied in support of her own achievements.

"Letters and pothooks, my dear Mrs. Herkimer? Muriel can read the newspapers and even 'Paradise Lost' perfectly well. She reads me to sleep every Sunday afternoon with 'Paradise Lost' or Young's 'Night Thoughts.' I think poetry is improving for the child, you know, and I enjoy it myself. It soothes me. And, by-the-way, it was she who wrote asking you to come here to-day."

"Well now! You don't——" ejaculated Martha; but Matilda, though mollified, ran on: "Indeed, I believe I have gained quite as much as Muriel by her lessons. One must know a thing in order to teach it. I found my own education had grown sadly rusty, and needed brushing up. I had no idea there was so much interesting information to be got from "Mangnall's Questions" and "The Child's History of England" till I went over them with Muriel. As to music, I used to play, but was getting out of practice; she has revived my interest in it, and now we both play and sing together—in a mild way, my dear Amelia; pray do not look apprehensive, I am not meditating an exhibition. But I was going to say, I think Muriel needs better teaching than mine, now; so we propose going to Montreal for the winter. I cannot teach languages, and her voice seems worth cultivating."

"Take her to Selby, Miss Matildy," cried the worthy Martha, little dreaming how her husband and his aunt wished her a lockjaw. "He is married to a sister of Judy's there—plays the organ at St. Wittikind's—does it beautiful, my dear, but you will have heard him—and if there is any sing in the child it is he will bring it out. He'd make the kettle sing."

"We can all do that," said Judith disgusted. "Put another stick in the stove, that's all it wants. And this is little Muriel's birthday, Miss Matilda? How old is she to-day? Twelve? Ah—Pretty child, but not very tall. But that is in the family, I suppose.

Dionysius is almost short, and Betsey there is really stumpy. But I do not see much resemblance in her to Betsey."

"Neither do I."

"But one would expect to see a family-likeness."

"Between second cousins? I do not see the necessity."

"Blood always tells, you know. Yet she is not even like Dionysius——no trace of his square intellectual forehead, or anything."

"Your niece and her uncle are Bunces, perhaps, and Muriel a Stanley."

"But she is not like you either."

"I confess I never was clever about seeing likenesses, but I am sure I could not be fonder of the child if she were ever so like me. Penelope, do you not think we might have tea, now?"

Considine had heard Martha's mention of Selby. It was the first time in years that he had heard the name. It awoke recollections which had long been asleep. Jordan, his co-trustee in the Herkimer fortune had no doubt told him the family story on his return to Montreal, but at that time his mind was full of his own cares, and since then the mere periodical investment of dividends had not called for a recurrence to the subject.

Though, doubtless, he remembered his old attachment, and would still have felt a kindness for its object had his thoughts wandered that way, the preoccupations of business led them in other directions; the tender passages were relegated to the same limbo as the memories of childhood, and his *ante bellum* possessions wiped out of existence by the event of war. Love-dreams, longings, the yearnings of what we call our "hearts," are luxuries of the well-to-do, living at their ease. When the wolf comes to the door, and the means of subsistence are in doubt or danger, Cupid, the ethereal sprite, feeding daintily on sighs and idle fancies, wings himself way; and in the turmoil of hard material facts, he is not missed. It is best so. The heart wounds, forgotten, skin over and heal, where head and arms are in danger from the blows of fortune ; and so the undivided energies are free for the combat.

But now, his personal affairs having arranged themselves in an easy well-to-do routine which gave no anxiety, his mind was open to other interests, and of these there were not enough to engage it. He often felt dull and lonely. He would now and then accompany Ralph to St. Euphrase, remaining over night and returning to town in the morning, thereby killing a long afternoon, as on the present occasion; but this could be only an occasional palliation. The "planting" years of his youth, as he called them, and the fighting years which followed, had not been the apprenticeship to make him take an undivided interest in business for its own sake after he had secured income sufficient for his needs. He had outlived his relish for the society of young men—young men of business, at least—the middle-aged had withdrawn into domestic life, and he found himself a good deal alone.

The mention of Selby's name stirred old associations which time and adventure had long deprived of bitterness; and now he looked back with only a plaintive yearning to the happiness which might have been, if he had had his way, and pitied himself in his solitary estate. If he had married, what wealth of love was his to have bestowed! And how he could have enjoyed being cosseted and purred to by a wife of his own, instead of depending on hirelings whose servile smile betrayed the hollowness of their attentions. The smoking-room at his club, and his own rooms at the hotel rose before his eye in their dull solid unsatisfying comfort, and he could not but compare them with the clean, unsmoky freshness and brightness of the woman's world around him, and confess the

15—2

two as different and apart as the close warm stuffiness of a winter sick-room, from the clear keen day out of doors in early spring.

" What ails you, gineral?   You look that glum you might have been hearing of your brother's death," said Martha, making room for him on the garden seat where she sat.

" I am well, madam.   I heard you allude just now to a Mr. Selby as having married the sister of Mrs. Bunce.   Are you acquainted with the lady?"

" To be sure I am.   She is Ralph's aunt. A dear good soul as ever lived, but real sorrowful-like and sickly now—she that used to be as peart and blooming as the flowers in May.   It's heart-breaking to see her.   She has never got over the loss of her child ten years ago, and it has fairly broke her up. Her hair is white like a woman of sixty.   She might be older than Judy, there; and yet she is just one age with Ralph—not forty yet."

" I recollect her very distinctly in her brother Gerald's lifetime—a beautiful young lady.   That was before the war; the first time I was in Canada."

" Were you in Canady then?   But to be sure you were!   You were Gerald's friend, and are a trustee of his property.   Ah, yes! I recollect.   And you were——"

But she did not say any more; only she looked in his face with a new interest, and what would have been a kind and sympathizing smile if good manners had not restrained the manifestation. Nothing awakens the interest of a good woman so warmly as a story of true enduring love. If the love have been unrequited, its constancy seems but the more rarely and touchingly beautiful. It is something to be dealt with delicately, and spoken to in low, soft, ambiguous words that may soothe but will not flutter the tender thing. It was such love that Martha dreamed of in her youth, and humbly hoped for; and when Ralph, young, eager and impetuous, found her in the New England homestead, she dreamed the divine influence had descended to stir the hushed and waiting waters of her life. She cheerfully left home and kindred to dwell with the man who loved her, and she had been his true and devoted wife. Yet often when she recalled the enthusiasm of that early time it seemed to her that the love-feast had been but a Barmecide's banquet after all, or like the husks with which another adventurer had to stay his hunger when he left the shelter of the paternal home. She lavished the wealth of her own affection, but the return had seemed but slender and humdrum to her high-

wrought expectations. The young couple
went to housekeeping, which is something
quite different from the life of the humming-
birds among the flowers: Love's dainty fare
of sighs and kisses gave place to the grosser
nourishment of bread and beef. The bread
had to be earned, the house had to be kept,
and very soon the pair of Arcadians found
themselves toilers like the rest of the world.
He toiled with a will, nay with a relish; it was
what he was better fitted for than the fantastic
joys of feeling ; and she did her part at least
without repining. It was what she had promised, and she did it loyally, if wearily at
times, in the colourless greyness of daily life,
when she recalled the rosy dawn of maiden
love, with the heavens above all shining, and
the world sparkling with dew. So Eve, may-
hap, looked back on Paradise when she was
sent forth with her lord into common life, and
doubtless she would sigh at times to remember
it, even with her boys growing up around her.
And so with Martha in her prosperity, to fancy
Considine cherishing the ashes of a blighted
love, stirred feelings not dead, but long since
grown to be a mere luxurious pain—a poig-
nancy of plaintive delight.

"Yes," said Considine, after allowing time
for the completion of Martha's interrupted

sentence, " yes, I believe it was to Miss Mary's adherence to her own choice in the matter of a husband that I owe my association with Jordan as trustee under that eccentric will. People cannot control their likings, I suppose, and I do think the young lady was hardly dealt with. I hope the marriage she was so set on has turned out well. Is she in good circumstances ? "

" They are very comfortable ; but not rich, of course. People do not make fortunes in Selby's profession ; but when a woman throws away one fortune she has no right to expect another. However they'd have done well enough if it had not been for losing the child. That has fairly broke them up. They live retired, and don't care to see anybody. Mary keeps her room half the time, and if it was not for Susan, who lives with them since Judy married, I don't know what they would do. But it gives me the dumps to think of them. Is this not a nice place, gineral? And how do you like the ladies? Seems to me Miss Matildy is just too altogether awful nice for anything."

And so she ran on, good soul. She was bent on withdrawing Considine from what she considered his " just too beautiful " contemplation of an ancient grief, and resolved to find him a suitable consoler. The consoler, indeed, was already fixed upon in her own mind, and ere she went home that afternoon, she had already begun to depict the interesting bachelor in colours which, but for the incipient baldness above his temples, the shaggy moustache, and the absence of wings, might have stood for the Cupid on an old-fashioned valentine.

Her auditor was quite interested, in a pleasant heart-whole way, and much as she might have been over a new variety of Brahmah or other fowl; for besides her lively sensibility, Matilda had a considerable fund of sober sense, though she was scarcely herself aware of it. Nevertheless, it *was* interesting to hear of the vanquished hero. Martha dwelt much on his warlike exploits, and his cherishing through years and battles the memory of his old attachment. Captain Lorrimer—who knew ?—might have done the same, and Matilda still thought kindly of him, though she had never read his name in any list of killed or wounded, and she had seen or heard nothing of him since he marched his men on board the steamer to the strains of "The girl I left behind me," amid the waving handkerchiefs of the ladies on the wharf; and henceforth Matilda felt very friendly and exerted herself to be pleasant whenever she found herself in Considine's company.

# CHAPTER XIII.

## ON ACCOUNT OF STRAWBERRIES.

THE tea-table was set on the lawn where the lengthening shadows inscribed themselves map-wise in islands and peninsulas of coolness; and within the opened windows on the verandah were other refreshments, whither the gentlemen were invited to bend their steps, while the ladies with their ices remained out of doors. Muriel looking up, saw Pierre disappearing among the bushes along the approach.

"Auntie," she whispered to Matilda, "give me a big heaped-up plate of strawberries and ice-cream for poor Pierre. See, there he goes away home, all by himself. How lonely he must feel! and hot, and thirsty, to see us all sitting out here eating nice things. Quick! Tilly, dear, or he will be through the gate, and at his own door before I can catch him; and then I may meet Annette, who is never nice to me. I don't like Annette."

The plate was speedily filled and heaped up, and away she ran.

To Pierre, trudging along the gravel in his heavy boots, the light footsteps in pursuit were inaudible ; and it was not till passing the gate, he stopped to close it behind him, that he heard his name called, and looking up, saw Muriel running towards him. Of course he stopped, and of course, too, being French, and a civil lad, he pulled off his cap and waited. An English lad would probably have turned back to meet the young mistress; but Pierre was apt to grow confused when Muriel appeared suddenly, she was so airy and different from his own heavy lumbering self. So there he stood, stock still like Jack stepping off his bean-stalk, when the fairy tripping down the meadow from the giant's castle, accosted him.

"Here, Pierre, I have brought you these. I wish I had seen you to give them sooner. You could have eaten them in the garden then, which would have been nicer."

"Oh! mademoiselle ees too kind," mumbled Pierre, reddening to the roots of his hair and looking sheepishly grateful. "Too moosh of trouble to give mademoiselle," and the burning black eyes looked out from under their lashes as if they would have spoken things forbidden to the stammering tongue. But there came a shrill call up the road just then, "Pier-r-re!" which quenched their lustre in a moment, and brought a faint frown of impatience even to Muriel's sunny brow.

"Your mother is calling you, Pierre. Good night. *Bon appétit.*"

"Ah! *coquin!* What is it thou dost there?" was the greeting which met him as he drew near, from his mother standing in the road before the door. "*Cochon! Bête!* And thou lingerest at the gate with the *donzelle*, forsooth. Thou!—Deny it not! Undutiful! And I have beaten thee for it when thou wert small, till my poor heart ached more than the bruises on thy little skin. And still thou wilt persist. I pray the heavenly queen upon my knees, and all the saints, to let thee die sooner than come to love her. 'Twere mortal sin."

"My mother? Calm yourself. It was only that the demoiselle ran after me to give this plate of fruit. Will you not taste it?"

"Taste gift of hers? *Enfante fausse!*" and she pushed aside the offered strawberries which rolled plentifully from the plate and were scattered on the ground."

"Ah, no, my mother! Not false! The youngest angel in heaven is not more true and

good than Mademoiselle Muriel. But you will
not think so—I remind me often how you beat
me for her sake. Beat me again, my mother,
if so it please you ; but she is good and very
beautiful."

" *Sacr-ré !* " she ground out from between
her clenched teeth, with flashing eyes glancing
up and down the road ; and then she started
with a sob of afright, and a tremor ran through
her frame as she composed herself to speak
quite calmly. " I see thy father coming home.
He must not know of what we have spoken, if
thou would'st have thy mother's blessing when
I die. Pick up thy berries. It was a heedless gesture of my arm which upset them.
Thou can'st say so much." And she went
indoors, leaving Pierre in bewilderment to
gather the fruit.

That his mother, so gentle and fond, so
sober, industrious and sensible, should break
out like one beside herself, if their ladies'
niece were but named, was unaccountable.
A mystery, and one he dared not even try to
solve. She had threatened to curse him if he
did but inquire. And yet it was only before
himself that she betrayed her feeling. In his
father's presence she showed no sign, but
would discuss the niece of their mistresses
with him with the same composure as their

horses, sheep or cattle. And yet mademoiselle was so sweet! And as he thought of her the bewilderment vanished in his mind like mist before the morning sun, and he forgot even to pick up his strawberries scattered around, while he knelt on the threshold.

"Heh, Pierre! On thy knees before sundown? Will the rosary not keep till bedtime?" said Jean, the father, stepping past him into the house.

"I am picking up some strawberries I let fall just now. Mademoiselle Muriel brought me them as I went home."

"She is an angel of considerateness and kindness—never forgets the poor for the sake of the rich—just like monsieur the general, her grandfather, if so please the ladies, and the demoiselles his daughters. A family most generous, even if they are not French and good Catholics;" and he crammed half-a-dozen large strawberries into his mouth at once, and gave them a crunch as though to drink the family's health in a bumper of strawberry wine.

Annette looked up from the baby she was nursing, and there was a gleam of red and smothered fire lurking in her eye, and she set her teeth tight to hold back the struggling wish that the girl's gift might choke him;

while sire and son seated themselves on the door-sill to consume the collation, the elder, at least, utterly unconscious that aught was amiss.

END OF VOL I.

www.ingramcontent.com/pod-product-compliance
Lightning Source LLC
Chambersburg PA
CBHW020106030726
47498CB00006B/1976

* 9 7 8 3 7 4 2 8 1 1 3 1 8 *